THE

SUBSTITUTE VICTIM

ALSO BY HUGH PENTECOST

THE

SUBSTITUTE

VICTIM

A Julian Quist Mystery Novel

Hugh Pentecost

Dodd, Mead & Company
New York

Published by Dodd, Mead & Company, Inc.
79 Madison Avenue, New York, N.Y. 10016
Distributed in Canada by
McClelland and Stewart Limited, Toronto
Manufactured in the United States of America

First Edition

Library of Congress Cataloging in Publication Data

Pentecost, Hugh, 1903–
    The substitute victim.

    I. Title.
PS3531.H442S8   1984   813'.52   84-13667
ISBN 0-396-08407-9

THE

SUBSTITUTE VICTIM

Part

ONE

1

The bombing of the Quatermayne was one of the most shocking acts of terrorism in the history of the city of New York. The old theater, west of Broadway in the Forties, recently bought and renovated by Duke Maxwell, sportsman, gambler, and entrepreneur, was blown to pieces a few minutes before curtain time for a preview performance of a new play. The death toll was staggering and included Maxwell himself, Elissa Hargrove, the famous film star making her Broadway debut, three other well-known actors who completed the cast of the play, the stage manager, a half a dozen stagehands, Miss Hargrove's maid-dresser, and the maid and dresser who worked for the character woman. These more than a dozen people, who were all backstage just prior to the rise of the curtain, were totally destroyed, some beyond recognition or identification. People in the first four rows of the audience were buried under tons of falling concrete and steel girders. The victims there included industrialist Warren Hargrove, the father of the star. His injuries, along with those of several others, were critical. The blazing fire that broke out sent the rest of a full house scrambling hysterically for the exits.

The noise of the explosion was so thunderous and earth-shaking in its effect that people streamed out of neighboring theaters, restaurants, hotels, and bars, most of them convinced that the dreaded nuclear attack from overseas had come at last. People who described the scene later spoke of seeing men and women staring up into the night sky, looking for the mushroom cloud that wasn't there. Firemen and their equipment, an army of policemen, people trying to get away, and others rushing in to gawk, jammed the streets.

Radios and television sets blared out the news. Famous people were dead: Elissa Hargrove had been destroyed in the holocaust; Warren Hargrove, her industrialist father was critically injured, not with much chance of survival. Tom Glidden, romantic leading man, was dead. So were Sarah Sampson and Jonathan Davies, two well-known character actors. Duke Maxwell, notorious owner of a vacation haven in Atlantic City, a professional football team, and the theater itself, had been blown to pieces. It would be hours before the complete list of dead and injured would be released.

Julian Quist, driving in from the country to his apartment on Beekman Place, heard the news on his car radio and pulled over to the side of the road to listen. Elissa Hargrove had been a client of his.

Quist, a tall, blond, handsome man in his late thirties, gripped the wheel of his car as he listened to a radio reporter on the scene trying to describe the disaster.

The reporter's voice was shaken, high pitched. "What is going on here is just beyond description. Dark smoke clouds dim the city lights. So far we are dealing mostly with rumors, all of them grim. It seems that everyone backstage at the Quatermayne was wiped out. You can't take it in when you say the words! Elissa Hargrove is dead! Duke Maxwell is dead, the millionaire sportsman and promoter who only recently made headlines by winning the big lottery—three and a half million dollars added to the many millions he already had. 'Them that has—gets!' the Duke remarked at the time. Tom Glidden, Sarah Sampson, Jonathan Davies—popular Broadway actors—all dead! All dead in one monstrous blast—aimed at whom, and for what reason? Facts and details about the many other casualties less well-known have yet to surface, but may help in a search for the answer to that question.

"It has been impossible to get anyone in authority to this microphone. Firemen are fighting to save what's left of the Quatermayne and the rest of the block; uniformed police are trying to control hysterical mobs of people. This kind of hysteria provides a field day for pickpockets, minor holdup men, and looters. Shop windows break, and nobody turns a head; all attention is focused on the burning theater. Elissa Hargrove will walk out through that cloud of black smoke! It can't be true! Elissa is immortal! The shock is what it might have been if someone had told your grandfather that Greta Garbo had been run down by a hit-and-run driver. Just not possible!"

The reporter stopped, coughing as a result of smoke inhalation, Quist thought. The man was right. It was impossible to take in. Elissa Hargrove *was* immortal—and the other famous people listed as dead. Grief for them would be paraded before the public for weeks to come, but it was no less a horror for the friends and families of the less prominent lost in the explosion.

"I'm sorry, ladies and gentlemen, but the air in this part of town is clogged with smoke and dust," the reporter continued. "Most of the firemen and police are wearing oxygen masks. The rest of us are not so lucky. I just had a few words with Captain Ed Stewart of the bomb squad, waiting for a chance to get inside the burning building. Captain Stewart assured me this was not the result of a letter bomb sent to someone in the theater. 'Not something sent as a box of chocolates,' he told me. 'This was a giant explosion, rigged, in advance, undoubtedly set off by remote control.

The man who set it off is probably blocks away, listening to you on the radio.' That is all the solid information we have so far. Dozens of people are being carried out of the Quatermayne to waiting ambulances. So far we have no information as to who they are or how badly they are hurt. It is sickening and beyond explanation so far, ladies and gentlemen."

Quist was suddenly aware that someone was standing outside the window on the driver's side of his car looking in.

"Something wrong, mister?"

It was a state trooper, the red light on the roof of his car blinking just behind him.

"I—I've just heard about the bombing in New York," Quist said. "Some of the people killed were friends of mine. I needed a few moments to get hold of myself. I've got to get back to town in case I can be helpful."

"You know Elissa Hargrove?" the trooper asked.

"Well."

"Brother! I can give you a guided tour as far as the toll booths at the Triborough—if you're up to following me."

"Thanks, officer."

The trooper went back to his car, the siren started to whine in the night. For the next twenty miles, Quist found himself driving at a speed he'd never attempted before. The toll booths loomed up ahead, and the red lights on the rear of the trooper's car began to blink as he slowed to a stop.

"Thanks," Quist called out as he pulled up alongside.

"Good luck," the trooper called back.

Quist knew that he was going to need more than luck to help friends who had been the victims of the Quatermayne tragedy.

Julian Quist lived in a duplex apartment on Beekman Place that he shared with a lady, a very special lady. Lydia

Morton was a writer and researcher for Julian Quist Associates, located in a glass finger pointing to the sky on Park Avenue, just north of Grand Central Station. Lydia had become a part of the scheme of things there through the recommendation of a mutual friend of hers and Julian's. She hadn't met the "head man" until the day she reported for work, but that day had changed both her life and his. It had been like throwing a switch and turning on a brilliant light. She and Julian were made for each other, and they had known it almost simultaneously and immediately. After five years they had become like one, living together, sharing both their business and social lives, and their most intimate love life—without marriage.

"It was so good right from the beginning," Quist told his friend Dan Garvey, "that we don't dare change it! Anything added or subtracted might throw it out of balance."

Quist needed his lady that evening, and she was where she should be when he let himself into their apartment. He took her in his arms when she came to the door to greet him. Neither of them spoke for a moment.

Quist finally held her away from him. "I was in a panic, love," he said. "I had a ghastly feeling you might be among the missing."

"I know how you felt," she said. "I wondered if you might have stopped at the Quatermayne on your way home!" They embraced again. "The phone has been going every minute. The fact that we've been handling Elissa's publicity isn't a secret. Every reporter in town has been calling to ask for information about her."

"Poor mixed-up lady," Quist said. "They think she was the main target?"

"You pays your money, and you takes your choice," Lydia said. "You need a drink." She headed for the bar at the far end of the living room to pour a Jack Daniels on the rocks. "How much have you heard, Julian?"

"Car radio. I picked it up in the middle of an on-the-spot

7

report." Quist took the whiskey she brought him and drank gratefully. "As the man on the TV commercial says, 'I needed that!'"

"One of the people who called was Pat Walsh."

"Irish clown," Quist said.

"But a first-rate reporter," Lydia said. "By some coincidence he was at the theater, sitting near the back, fortunately. He wasn't hurt."

"He never lets up on the Hargroves, does he?"

"It's a way to eat," Lydia said. "He was there—and so was Warren Hargrove, sitting in the front row right under where the roof collapsed."

"Is there any report on him?"

"Critical, in the hospital. Hasn't been able to talk, and the word is he may never be able to."

The phone was ringing, and Lydia answered it. "Mark!" she said. "Hold on." She held out the phone to Quist. "Mark Kreevich," she said.

Lieutenant Mark Kreevich of Manhattan Homicide was an old and trusted friend of Quist's and Lydia's. They had known each other both professionally and socially over the years. Mutual pleasure in one another's company plus respect for each other's competence in his own field made for strong ties. Not infrequently Quist had been helpful to Kreevich on one of his cases, and Kreevich had often been helpful to Quist on one of his big promotions.

"Mark!" Quist said, as he picked up the phone.

"You know what's going on down here at the Quatermayne?" the detective asked. His voice was cold, distant, almost hostile.

"Car radio, as I was driving in from the country," Quist said. "Nothing too solid."

"There is nothing solid yet—except the list of the dead," Kreevich said. "Elissa Hargrove was a client of yours, wasn't she?"

"I never thought I'd hear the word 'was' in connection with her."

"She has to be considered a primary target, Julian—she and her father. I've never paid too much attention to all the gossip about her, but now I have to. Can you help?"

"I guess—at the office—we have every word that's ever been printed about her."

"Useful, but there isn't time now to do an all-night study," Kreevich said. "You and Lydia can probably tell me enough to get me started, files later. Can you come down here, both of you?"

"Of course."

"We've got a temporary headquarters set up in the Benson Hotel across the street from the theater. Ask for me. Don't get sidetracked by anyone else. This is a madhouse down here."

"Madhouse" was an inadequate word to describe the state of things in the area surrounding what was left of the Quatermayne Theater. The taxi that Quist and Lydia took from their apartment couldn't get them closer than two blocks from the disaster. Police had closed off traffic, except for fire trucks, ambulances, and other official vehicles. Crowds of people seemed to be hurrying in all directions at once. Some of them had the look of greed for excitement; others appeared to be in shock from what they had seen.

When they reached the street where the Quatermayne and the Benson Hotel were located, they were stopped by police. Fire hoses blocked the street, and rivers of water ran down the gutters. Smoke still billowed toward the sky. Quist had some difficulty persuading a cop, angry from turning away persistent sightseers, that he was answering a summons from Lieutenant Kreevich. They were provided with a uniformed escort and a warning that, if this was "some sort of gag," they'd spend the night in jail.

It was hard to believe the almost total destruction of the

theater when they reached it. The marquee and the front doors were a mass of broken glass. Down the alley, between buildings, they could see the total destruction of the rear of the theater.

The lobby of the hotel was jammed with people, many of whom Quist knew by sight—reporters, TV cameramen. Those who knew Quist and his connection with Elissa Hargrove tried to block their way, shouting questions. The uniformed escort managed to run interference for them and got them to a private dining room at the rear of the lobby that had been set up as an office for the police. At the far end of the room, Lieutenant Kreevich was sitting at a table talking to a man Quist didn't know. Other policemen and officials were interviewing other people. A cop at the door took the message to Kreevich, who looked up, glanced at his friends as though they were strangers, and gestured for them to be brought in.

"Mark looks as though he'd really had it," Lydia said.

Kreevich, tall, slim, dark, usually with a friendly smile, was grim-faced.

"You know Fred Vail?" he asked, as Quist and Lydia reached the table. "He's Duke Maxwell's lawyer and business manager."

Vail was a small, neatly dressed man with thinning brown hair and a neat little mustache over a mouth that was a tight slit. A man fighting for control, Quist thought.

"I know who you are, of course, Mr. Quist," he said. He acknowledged an introduction to Lydia with a curt little nod. "Your friend, Dan Garvey, used to play for Duke, you know."

"Nobody who was in that hell makes very much sense yet," Kreevich said.

"You were there?" Quist asked Vail.

"In the box office, out of the danger area," Vail said. "When the bomb went off, three of us who were in the box office were knocked to the floor—luckily, not hurt."

"Duke wasn't with you?" Quist asked.

"He was in the lobby, greeting friends. This was to have been a preview performance, you know. Lot of paper in the house, free seats. One of the ushers tells us Duke got a message that he was wanted backstage. Just after he got there, the whole place blew up."

"What was he wanted for?" Quist asked.

"No one left alive to tell us," Kreevich said, his voice harsh. "Everyone backstage was wiped out."

"But you know for certain Duke Maxwell was there, and Elissa?" Quist asked.

"Not from being able to identify individual pieces of meat," Kreevich said. He glanced at Lydia. "Sorry for talking tough, Lydia, but you wouldn't believe what it's like back there." He nodded toward the theater across the street.

"Hands, arms, legs scattered around," Vail said, "with no way to guess what torso they belong to. Heads blown off shoulders, intestines scattered around like spaghetti—"

"Stop it!" Kreevich said.

"It's all right, Mark," Lydia said.

"It's *my* stomach that's queasy. I've seen it!" Kreevich said. He turned to Vail. "That list of people who may have had it in for the Duke—? I'd appreciate it if you and your staff would put it together for me as quickly as possible."

"Sure," Vail said. He stood up. "You can't imagine what my office will be like, a thousand people who owe the Duke, a thousand people he owes."

"He had financial troubles?" Kreevich asked.

"Hell, no!" Vail said, his laugh mirthless. "He can't go to jail for it now, and it will be all over the news media. He covered bets from big time gamblers from coast to coast. And he wasn't a loser."

"Until tonight," Kreevich said. "That list, Mr. Vail—?"

"Take a month to complete it," Vail said, "but I'll give you something to start on in an hour." He nodded to Quist and

Lydia and went out into the hall. As the door opened and closed, they were inundated by a cacophony of excited voices.

Kreevich leaned back in his chair and, for a moment, pressed the tips of his fingers against his eyelids. "Don't go over there," he said to his friends. "It's horrorville."

"You think this was aimed at Duke Maxwell?" Quist asked.

"A prime possibility," Kreevich said. "It was his property that was destroyed, his was one of the lives that was taken."

"What about the message that took him backstage?" Quist asked.

"He was talking with friends in the lobby," Kreevich said. "One of the ushers came to him and told him he was needed backstage. Not why—in anyone's hearing. Duke and the usher went backstage together. Both blown to bits."

"Maybe he was just being told it was time to go backstage and wish the cast luck," Lydia suggested. "What is it they say—'break a leg'?"

"Maybe it was to make sure he was back there when someone pressed the button that set off the bomb," Kreevich said.

"So why did you send for us, Mark?" Quist asked. "We've never had any dealings with Duke Maxwell. Oh, I knew him, had a drink with him here and there, but I didn't really *know* him. Vail's right, of course, Dan knows him."

"What we've got is a broken building, broken bodies, but only the vaguest starting points to take us to who and why," Kreevich said. "There were four very controversial people killed in that explosion—maybe more that I haven't caught up with yet."

"Controversial?" Lydia asked.

"People who might be targets for terrorism," Kreevich said. "Duke Maxwell had connections with gamblers and the underworld. He could have been the main target, with the violence of the attack meant as a warning to anyone else who crossed the wrong hoodlums."

"But why the slaughter of so many innocent people?" Lydia asked. "They could have bombed his theater when there was no one in it. It would have cost Maxwell just as much. You can hire someone to kill a man without destroying so many and attracting all the top investigators in the country!"

"That's one of the teasers," Kreevich said. "Does someone want us to think he was after Duke Maxwell, when he was really after someone else? For example, there is Mike Naylor, a guy who had a lot of clout in IATSE, a man who will trade you violence for violence, if you give him a chance."

"What is IATSE?" Lydia asked.

"Stagehands' union," Kreevich told her. "It's the International Association of Theater and Stage Employees—something like that. Naylor was a rough, tough guy that many people in the theater will be glad to have out of their hair."

"He was working at the Quatermayne?" Quist asked.

"Head electrician. Even in a small cast play like this was, you have a head electrician, a head carpenter, wardrobe, curtain operator, and on and on—all required to be members of the union. Unions guarantee jobs, but, who knows, maybe they cost them, too. You must hire this one, or that one, whether you need him or not. Makes everything too damned expensive!"

"So Mike Naylor had enemies?" Quist asked.

"Anyone who goes around telling you what you have to do has enemies."

"Which brings us, I take it, to Elissa Hargrove," Quist said.

"I thought you'd never guess!" Kreevich said, sounding

almost bitter. "Here is a lady whom all America watched, day by day, hour by hour. Who did she have dinner with? Did she go to bed with him? Did she also have breakfast with him? Don't ever let her have any privacy, any peace."

"Which is not what makes her controversial," Quist said.

"Politics," Kreevich said. "Almost everyone in the world discusses politics for a short time each day, and yet almost nobody knows anything about politics. You root for the home team, right or wrong, winning or losing. When you don't root for the home team, you are a spy, a traitor, a villain."

"And Elissa hasn't always rooted for the home team," Quist said.

"A beautiful blonde, who is constantly rooting for dark-skinned, sinister-looking Arabs! Every time she opens her mouth, she puts her foot in it. Arafat! That Prince Charming of the Palestinians!"

"The problem is," Quist said, "that, every time she does open her mouth, there is someone listening or focusing a camera on her. You and I probably make just as many statements that would be objected to by the majority, only the press isn't listening."

"Let's continue this fascinating discussion of social ills some other time. Elissa Hargrove has made headlines with her political statements. She is pro-Arab, which makes her anti-the United States marines! It also makes her anti-Semitic! There are passionate Zionists who would want to see her silenced. There may be Arab terrorists who have decided that, while hobnobbing with their big shots, she has come up with information it isn't safe for her to have. Most of all, her influence on her father could be disastrous for some people in power."

"You're suggesting she can pull Warren Hargrove around by the nose?" Quist asked.

"Look at it for a moment as though you hadn't known

them," Kreevich said. "Here is Warren Hargrove, millionaire manufacturer of high technology armaments—guns, planes, nuclear gimmicks. We know the Pentagon is one of his big customers. But, when you make something to sell, you have to find a market for it. Will Ford not sell in Volkswagen country? And vice versa? So this man has a glamorous, movie-star daughter who shoots off her mouth about what most of us think of as 'the enemy.' Has she persuaded her old man to sell weapons to Arafat, or Syria, or some fanatical Khomeini? Or has he always supplied the other side and persuaded his daughter that 'those other people' aren't so bad? Whichever way it worked, Elissa and her poppa can be dangerous to us, dangerous to Israel, dangerous to revolutionary elements in the countries they may be helping. Those two are controversial up to here!" Kreevich made a gesture toward his throat.

Quist was silent for a moment. "So what do you expect from me, Mark?" he asked.

"Somewhere there must be a file on Elissa Hargrove," Kreevich said. "Who her real friends are, her private-private attachments."

"Meaning lovers?"

"Or girl friends—if she's queer!"

"I think you can write that one off," Quist said. "Unless she's ambidextrous."

"I need to get hold of something in a hurry," Kreevich said. "The FBI and the CIA probably have travel records and political histories of both father and daughter. But it's going to be sticky getting hold of them quickly. Everyone will want to come out of this night smelling of roses. Any special advantage one group may have, they'll be slow in passing on to another. I need something that will get me out of the starting blocks, Julian. The other night, when I stopped in at your apartment, you told me you were doing a job on Elissa Hargrove. I took it to mean promoting this new play, and I didn't give it a second thought. Was that it?"

"Not exactly," Quist said. "Duke Maxwell had his own promo people—and good ones. A new play by Jeb Carleton is news; Elissa's Broadway debut is news. That was enough in itself to promote any theatrical venture."

"And your job?" Kreevich asked.

"To counter any adverse campaign against Elissa. Make her a friend of Jewish charities; Christmas fund raising for our troops abroad; a whole series of patriotic, pro-American appearances."

"Who hired you for this whitewash job?" Kreevich asked.

"Elissa."

Kreevich leaned forward. "She hired you herself, to make her look like something she wasn't?"

Quist's mouth tightened. "Everytime you say 'was,' I feel a fresh shock," he said. "'Elissa was—' *Is,* damn it!"

"Sorry, friend," Kreevich said. "Tell me what you can about the lady. If she hired you to clean her up, she must have told you where some of the dirt was."

Lydia interrupted. "I've been putting together a file on Elissa for Julian, Mark—at the office. Why don't I get it while Julian tells you what he can? It's clippings, biography, the works."

"Bless you," Kreevich said.

The lieutenant and Quist were alone at the table. There was the babble of voices in the lobby as Lydia left the room.

"It will take her a while—just to get out of here and back in," Quist said.

"Hold it," Kreevich said. "I'll supply her with a police car and someone to get her out and in."

Quist sat still at the table, going back in his mind to the time some days ago when Elissa had made an appointment to see him at his apartment. She hadn't wanted to come to his office, because she was concerned about anyone knowing she intended to engage him to work for her.

"If word gets out that you're working for me, no one will believe what you set up for me," she'd said.

"If I set anything up," he'd said. "I haven't agreed yet to do anything for you."

So she'd come to his apartment, with Lydia present. He hadn't known what to expect. He had never tried to sell something in which he didn't personally believe, and he wasn't at all sure that he believed in Elissa Hargrove. Way back in the McCarthy days, movie personalities had been branded Communist if they expressed a personal opinion that opposed a conservative view of things. Elissa had done a lot of unpopular talking in the last couple of years, and she was a big enough star for it to have hurt her in the media.

Quist, whose work brought him into contact with most of the top people in the entertainment world, had never seen Elissa Hargrove, except on the screen, until that evening at his apartment. Any makeup man can do wonders for a female star on camera. Quist thought nothing could have been done to improve the stunning beauty of the golden-haired woman who came to his apartment that evening. What surprised him was that her screen personality had suggested a confident, controlled, completely in command woman. What he confronted at the front door of his apartment was someone uncertain, even fearful, in need of help.

"Thank you for being willing to see me here, Mr. Quist," she said.

"It's a pleasure to see the real person," he said.

Lydia was introduced. Elissa wasn't interested in a drink, but accepted the coffee Lydia offered.

"You probably have some opinion about me that I wouldn't enjoy," Elissa said to Quist when they were settled before the fireplace in the living room.

"If you mean I probably believe everything I read, you're wrong," Quist said. "I help to develop stories in the press, which makes me a little cynical about what I see there."

"You know that I'm about to open in a Broadway play, *Undertow*, by Jeb Carleton?"

"And produced by Duke Maxwell," Quist said.

"It's something I want to go well more than anything I've ever been involved with. I've dreamed of the theater ever since I was a kid. I've had all kinds of good luck in films, good directors, good casts, good stories. They made me, I didn't make them. But now—well, I've got to be good, I've got to be accepted by the public. Just being here—on Broadway—all the negative things that have ever been said about my so-called politics are being revived. No matter how good the play is, no matter how good I am, the whole thing may go down the drain because of that."

"Duke Maxwell has top flight publicity people working for him."

"I question that, Mr. Quist. The old 'as long as you spell my name right' doesn't work for me. They spell my name right, but, as long as they say the wrong things about me, it isn't going to work."

"How honest are you prepared to be with me?" Quist asked.

She looked at him, surprised. "Honest?"

"There is an image of you that you want to sell," Quist said, "and there is the image of you created by the press. And then there is the real you. I meant, how honest can you be about that real you?"

"I don't think I'm a phony, Mr. Quist," she said, after a brief silence. "What I say, privately or publicly, is what I really think. I don't put on an act for anybody."

"An actress who doesn't act?"

"Unless I have a script to follow."

Quist smiled at her. "And 'the real you' writes her own script?"

"I learned too late that, if you are a public personality, you can't be yourself," Elissa said. "I say what I think; someone else interprets it and says I said something else. Pat Walsh, who writes for a big news syndicate, has been making a living misinterpreting me and my father."

"You mean you are *not* a friend of Mr. Arafat and the Palestine Liberation Organization?"

"Oh my, oh my, that jerk!"

"Arafat?"

"Pat Walsh! I have said, publicly, that Washington is making a mistake not negotiating with Arafat. The PLO will not agree that Israel has a right to exist. Until they change that, Washington won't talk. When I say they should talk, Pat Walsh writes that I am an enemy of the Jewish people! I'm no such thing! I'm against the notion that anyone can get anywhere without talking! What is it Mrs. Ghandi says? 'You can't make friends with a clenched fist'?"

"So, thanks to Pat Walsh and others, Jewish organizations threaten to boycott your play?"

"Thanks to Pat Walsh, I am an anti-Semite, pro-Arab, my father sells weapons to the Syrians, who shoot at our marines—and on, and on. Don't you believe we should talk to the enemy, try to settle our differences with them before someone launches the first nuclear attack?"

"Yes, I do."

"Don't say so in public. You'll be accused of being a Communist."

"Does Pat Walsh have anything personal against you?" Quist asked.

"That jerk! Yes, he does. He once made a pass at me, and I turned him off in a rather public way. He's the elephant who will never forget!"

"And your father?"

"His name is Hargrove. He's very rich, which is a sin, I guess. He has dealings with powerful men all over the world, which is sinister. He's my father, which makes him all bad in Mr. Walsh's eyes."

"Your father could put Walsh out of business if he wanted to."

"My father laughs at him. But my father isn't going to appear in a play and doesn't need audiences to love him. Will you help me, Mr. Quist?"

He hadn't hesitated. "Yes, I think I will," he'd told her. "Anyone who will send Mr. Patrick A. Walsh packing deserves a friend."

Quist described that encounter to Lieutenant Kreevich when the detective rejoined him.

"You sound as if you're not very fond of Pat Walsh yourself," Kreevich said.

"He's a reporter who uses the story he's covering to promote himself and not the story," Quist said.

"He's out there in that mob in the lobby now," Kreevich said.

"Probably not very happy. Losing Elissa has cost him a breadwinner."

"But the lady was very vocal about politics."

"Elissa had a very special upbringing," Quist said. "Her mother died when she was three or four years old. She traveled the world with her father. She grew up talking to people in power—prime ministers, presidents, royalty, power people. World affairs went with the breakfast coffee. She's always talked more about them, because they personally interested her, and she knew more about them than most people. I found her views quite sensible, reasonable, and without prejudice. But an actress doesn't have a right to have opinions, it seems."

"Did her father always go to all her performances, previews included?"

"I don't know. Elissa never talked about it. This was her

first important stage appearance in years. From things she said, I think Warren Hargrove was very proud of his daughter, but whether he could have been counted on to be present tonight, I don't know."

"It's a mess, Julian," Kreevich said. "It may have had nothing to do with the Hargroves at all. Someone may have been the target we haven't even thought of yet. Most of the people who might know are dead. A mess in spades!"

"No witnesses who claim to have seen anything?"

"People who ran out of there claim to have seen everyone from President Reagan to Princess Diana in the house," Kreevich said, an edge of anger in his voice. "Hundreds of phone calls from people who 'think' someone they knew may have been there."

"Can't Vail and the other box office people come up with a list of reservations for tickets?"

"They're trying to put together a list. No famous names so far. The target may not have been anyone famous. A crazy man wouldn't care who he killed as long as he got the person he was after."

The outer door opened again, to the clamor of voices, and closed behind an impressive-looking man in a business suit and a younger man wearing blue jeans and a work shirt.

"Thought I'd bring you up-to-date, Lieutenant," the man in the business suit said.

Kreevich introduced Captain Stewart of the bomb squad, explaining who Quist was and his connection with Elissa Hargrove.

"Sorry for you—and a couple of hundred other people who've lost someone," Stewart said. "This is Phil Guardino, an electrician who got lucky. He was supposed to be backstage but he wasn't."

Guardino made a comic little gesture of thanks to the heavens. "Mike Naylor asked me to get him some coffee before the curtain went up. I was across the street at the lunch counter when the whole place blew up. Someone was watching over me."

"To add to what I've already told you, Kreevich," Captain Stewart said, "this wasn't just a bomb tossed into the place. We're beginning to guess there may have been three bombs, rigged to go off together; one certainly set behind the light board on the left of the stage."

"Stage right, if you're an actor or someone who works back of the curtain," Guardino said.

"One set there," Stewart said, "one at the rear of the stage near the dressing rooms. And one in the ceiling in front of the stage."

"That's at the very top of the building," Guardino said. "First balcony, second balcony before you hit the ceiling."

"Full impact of explosion in those three places. We think, at the moment, that somehow it was expertly all hooked into the light board, which Mike Naylor was operating. When he pulled the lever, or whatever, that dimmed the house lights, just before the curtain was supposed to go up, that set off all three bombs."

"You're saying Naylor set off the explosion that killed him?" Kreevich asked.

"And everyone else."

"You think Naylor may have known—?"

"No way!" Guardino said. His short, sharp laugh was bitter. "No one wanted to be alive and kicking more than Mike. And I mean 'kicking.' Headed for top spot in our union, happy in a perpetual fight with management. Had a girl that would make your mouth water!"

"Someone had to know the whole electrical system to set up a thing like Captain Stewart describes," Kreevich said.

"That's why I brought Guardino here, a quiet place where I could go into that," Stewart said.

"I was across the street in the coffee shop when it blew," Guardino said. "You've got witnesses to that."

"Maybe you knew when to be missing," Stewart said.

"Oh, come on, Captain!"

"Did anyone hear Naylor ask you to get coffee for him?" Stewart asked.

"Sure. Bob Bowman, the curtain operator, was standing right there. Asked me to bring him some, too."

"But he's dead, along with Naylor. He can't verify your story. Wouldn't you have been needed backstage when the curtain was about to go up?"

"No," Guardino said. "You want me to tell you what the routine is again?"

"Please. Once more, for the lieutenant," Stewart said. He was suddenly an accuser.

Guardino spoke with a kind of exasperation. "I've told you and told you!" he said. "So, here we go once more. The curtain for a preview performance is at eight o'clock. The heads of all departments—electrical, carpenter, props, wardrobe, and the rest turn up at five-thirty. The electrical boss, who is Mike Naylor, checks out lights. The curtain operator checks out the curtain. Everybody checks everything. No bomb was connected to any of those things, or it would have blown up an hour and a half before it did. The rest of the crew comes in at six-thirty, along with the actors and other backstage people."

"That included you?" Stewart asked.

"Yes."

"And what was your job when you came in?"

"I report to Mike. If anything has gone wrong in the testing, I'm there to help with any repairs or adjustments."

"And there had been nothing out of order tonight?"

"Everything go," Guardino said.

"Then the bomb or bombs couldn't have been attached to the light board," Kreevich said.

"That doesn't follow," Stewart said. "After the testing at five-thirty or a quarter to six, all someone had to do was to connect a wire at the back of the light board. The next time the proper lever was pulled, off it would go."

"And you think it could have been me," Guardino said. "You think I invented the coffee story so I'd be out of the way?"

"It could have been you," Stewart said. "It could have been anyone who was in the theater after the lights had been tested."

"A stranger who got in?" Kreevich suggested.

"No way," Guardino said. "There's a guard at the stage door; the front of the house is locked until it's time for the audience to be admitted. From six-thirty on, I was around the light board most of the time. There wasn't anyone who didn't belong."

"We can't ask if anyone else saw anyone," Stewart said, "because they're all dead—except this man who went for coffee."

"A question," Kreevich said, after a moment of silence. "As you describe three connecting bombs, carefully put in place, it couldn't have been set up casually or in a hurry, could it?"

"I would think not," Stewart said.

"Take some time? Half an hour, an hour?"

"I'd guess that."

"So the theater was empty all day. Someone got in, took his time, came back later to connect a wire after the testing."

"Could be," Stewart said, frowning. "As a matter of fact, the bombs could have been put in place days ago. No real danger until the connection was made that would trigger them when the right lever was pulled or button pressed."

"Take some skill and knowledge, right?"

"To make the bombs, put them in just the right places to do the most damage," Stewart said. "But almost anyone could have made that final connection behind the board, given instructions."

"Anyone," Guardino said, "—and not know what he was doing?"

"And wouldn't ask questions if Naylor asked him to do it, or you asked him, Guardino," Stewart said.

Guardino squared his shoulders and faced the bomb squad man. "You having fun, Captain, trying to fit me into a puzzle that hasn't got any other pieces?"

"No other pieces alive," Stewart said.

"Who did I want to get?" Guardino demanded, his face darkening with anger. "Did I want to get Mike Naylor's job from him? Well, there's no job left! Did I have it in for Duke Maxwell? A labor war? All I had to do was catch up with him in the side alley, coming or going, not kill two dozen other people. Blowing up his theater wouldn't hurt him if he was dead. Was I trying to get even with some broad who said 'no' to me? I commit a mass murder to get even for that? Come up with a motive, Captain, or stop pointing at me! You hate me because I got lucky and was across the street?"

Quist broke a long silence. "While you're waiting for Lydia to come back with our file on Elissa, Mark," he said to his detective friend, "would it be wasting time to talk to Pat Walsh? You say he's out in the lobby. He's made a life's work of the Hargroves, father and daughter."

Guardino, still under a head of steam, faced them. "Why don't you two make-believe cops stop playing guessing games and come up with something solid?"

Kreevich was on his feet, standing close to the young electrician, a hand closed on his arm. "So help us!" he said. "You're the only one left alive who can give us information about that backstage area."

"And if I don't choose to?"

"You'll find yourself under arrest, suspected of mass murder," Kreevich said. "Let's take a walk."

2

Quist found himself left behind in the private rooms. Other interrogations were taking place away from the table Kreevich had occupied. Murder was not a new experience for Quist, but this was not like anything else he'd ever encountered. No witnesses left alive; nothing for ballistics to deal with; nothing for Stewart and the bomb squad to get their teeth into, except wreckage where the main impact of the bombs had taken place; nothing for the police photographers, except mangled bodies and a destroyed building. Perhaps, in time, these experts would come up with bits and pieces that would total something. But the key lay in the life of just one of the people who had died in the blast. Elissa? Her father? Duke Maxwell? Mike Naylor? Someone they hadn't even thought about yet?

The door to the lobby opened again. Nothing had quieted out there. A cop brought in a young man wearing a dark blue, tropical worsted, summer suit with a bright navy-and-red polka-dot tie. He had blue eyes, narrowed against the bright lights in the room, and his smile was forced as he started toward Quist.

"I'm Pat Walsh," he said.

"I know," Quist said.

"Kreevich flagged me in the lobby and said you might be interested in talking to me. We have a mutual interest in what's happened here."

"Elissa."

"And her father," Walsh said. "Kreevich says you're about to present him with a file on Elissa. Maybe I can add to it."

"From what I've read of yours, Walsh, I don't doubt that you can add to it. You got lucky tonight."

"You mean that I was sitting at the back of the theater?"

"That was luck, wasn't it? Or did you know where to sit in safety?"

"If that's the way you want to play it, there's not much use talking, is there?" Walsh said.

"For more than two years you've been hounding Elissa with accusations, innuendos, falsehoods," Quist said.

"Why didn't she sue me and the syndicate that publishes me?"

"Perhaps because it would only focus attention on what you were saying about her," Quist said.

"Did she tell you that I might have personal reasons for hounding her?"

"That you made a pass at her and that she managed to ridicule you, publicly, in some fashion?"

Walsh nodded. "It's true," he said. "I had no reason to love her for that. But my job as a reporter had nothing to do with it."

"Colored it a little, perhaps?"

Walsh held a lighter to a cigarette, squinting at Quist through the smoke. "You handle all kinds of temperamental and offbeat people in your business, Quist. Do you do a less good job for them if you don't happen to like them?" Walsh dropped the lighter back in his pocket. "I'm a reporter. My job is to unearth facts. How I feel personally about people I run into in the process doesn't color anything."

"You've been gunning for Elissa for about two years

now," Quist said. "That's a hell of a lot of vindictive gossip, Walsh."

"Do you think International, my news service, would pay me to carry on a personal vendetta?"

"If the subject was glamorous enough, famous enough."

Walsh took a deep drag on his cigarette. "Elissa is just the window dressing in the story that interests me," he said and let the smoke out in a long sigh.

"Meaning?"

"Do you give a damn, Quist, whether there is a world to wake up to tomorrow morning? Do you give a damn whether some jerk in Washington or Moscow presses a button that means the end of everything? Do you care if irresponsible, power-hungry industrialists sell high technology weapons to religious fanatics who are prepared to turn them right back on us and put out the sun, the moon, and the stars forever?"

"Pretty fancy talk, Walsh, but—yes, I care."

"He is a very smart, very devious, very complex man—Warren Hargrove," Walsh said. "On Mondays, I think Elissa was a co-conspirator with him. On Tuesdays, I think she was brainwashed by her old man into believing a lot of bullshit, so that he could use her to distract attention from his own actions." Walsh turned toward a window. "You been across the street yet?"

"Not inside," Quist said.

"Fanatical terrorism," Walsh said. "You kill an army to get one man—or woman. Anywhere else but in the United States people would understand what it was. A message! A warning! Jews warning Arabs, Arabs warning Jews, Iranians warning Iraqis and vice versa. Here we think it's just some crazy, hungry for blood and guts."

"And you think—?"

"I think it's a message to someone from someone, warning them not to do business with people like Warren Hargrove."

"Do business?"

"Selling weapons and high technology to anyone with oil-rich payoffs to make."

"You think Hargrove has been selling weapons to people we think of as enemies?"

"I *know* it," Walsh said, bringing the flat of his hand down hard on the table.

"Proof?"

"I've been two years trying to find something that would make our government listen!" Walsh said. "They buy from Hargrove. The Pentagon is one of his best customers. The proof has to be gold-plated before they will listen."

"But you 'know' it," Quist said.

"Everybody in the Middle East knows it," Walsh said. "They laugh at us behind our backs. Explosives and technology supplied by one of our own people could have slaughtered our marines in Lebanon."

"That's a pretty wild charge," Quist said. "Your articles have been mostly aimed at Elissa."

"She was a friend of the wrong people—the PLO, the Arabs who don't feel the Jews have any right to exist in Israel, the outspoken enemies of the Western powers. Her old man would laugh when questioned about her. 'Today's young revolutionaries,' he would say. But it gave him an excuse to go where she went, ostensibly to quiet her down, 'keep her from wrecking her film career.' What it did was to give him a chance to make his deals without attracting attention to himself."

"So, why were you at the theater tonight?"

"The Hargroves are—were—my business. I spent the day in Washington trying to persuade some lunkhead in the CIA to listen to what I had on Hargrove. They wear earmuffs down there if they don't want to hear what you have to say. I have a guy keeping track of Hargrove for me. I need to know if he takes off for someplace. I want to be there, see who he meets, who he talks with. When I got back from Washington about seven o'clock tonight, my guy told me that Hargrove was going to the Quatermayne to see his daughter act. The theater would be a place where he could meet someone, deal with someone."

"Was he that public?"

"Smart operator, like I said. Try to meet someone in secret, and he could be watched—our people, Israeli people. A casual meeting in a public place doesn't look like he was wheeling and dealing."

"You saw him in the theater?"

"Sure. Right down in the front row where he always sits. And then the roof fell in!"

"While you were safely at the back of the house."

"I don't go around sitting at his elbow," Walsh said. "I've been after him too long, and he knows it. If he spotted me, he'd start dancing to some other tune."

Over most of his adult years and all through his professional career, Quist had been listening to facts and fictions about people and their particular functioning. He had come to believe that he had an instinct for truth when he heard it. He had come to trust that instinct, and he found himself listening to Pat Walsh and abandoning the notion that this was all some wild invention of the young reporter's.

"Who else have you told this story to before tonight?" Quist asked.

"To start with, my managing editor at the news syndicate. He thinks enough of it to have given me the green light to stay with it. He's the only one who doesn't think I'm off my rocker. I told you I spent today talking to a high-up in the CIA. He just laughed at me. Hargrove is a fine, patriotic American! No way he would be helping the wrong people. Same response from the State Department and the Pentagon. Dump my garbage somewhere else, is their response."

"Two years you've been at it!" Quist said. "You must have

come up with some leads to people or organizations who might be responsible for what happened tonight."

Walsh made an impatient gesture. "Jews for Direct Action, Arabs for Arabs, Terror for the Hell of it! The woods are full of 'groups.' Individuals? In this day and age, Quist, you can hire a hit man, a bomb expert, a terrorist anywhere from Japan to East Germany. He does what he does, not for a cause, but for money."

"And the real killer sits in his luxury hotel suite, doing his crossword puzzle, while a man who cares only for the fee he'll be paid does the job?"

Walsh nodded.

"You have a list of suspects?" Quist asked.

"I'll tell you something, Quist," Walsh said. "If I had anything that was a hot lead, I wouldn't be here. All I need to convince me that I'm not close is that I'm still alive!"

"Is it worth the risk, just to get even with a lady who said 'no' to you in public?" Quist asked.

Walsh's smile had a kind of angry shine to it. "I like to think that any risks I'm running are for national security. I may regret that the lady didn't live long enough for me to take a second try at her. But who knows, what appeared to be sexy about her could just have been acting. Is she any good in the hay, Mr. Quist?"

"You should go somewhere and wash out your mouth with soap," Quist said.

In any large disaster like a fire, a plane crash, an earthquake, a ship sinking—anything that costs many lives—there are just as many stories as there are lives snuffed out, probably more. Warren Hargrove, buried under tons of cement and twisted steel, probably breathing his last in a hospital emergency ward, was almost certainly a story. But what about people across oceans with whom he dealt? His death would certainly affect their financial futures, their political positions, perhaps their social lives, their love lives, the lives of their children. Track down every lead to and from every person who had died in the bombing, and it would take a trained research staff forever to assemble it all—and more time, without extraordinary luck, to find a solid clue that would point to the person or persons who had bombed the Quatermayne, and their reasons and motives for doing it. The enormity of this chore explained why Lieutenant Kreevich and Captain Stewart, highly trained and skillful professionals, appeared to be walking in a daze. Where to begin?

"I suppose the best thing I can do is get out of your hair," Quist said to Kreevich, when the detective came back to the room in the hotel after taking Guardino backstage at the Quatermayne.

"You can help if you will," Kreevich said.

"How?"

"We have a list of forty-two people dead, plus seventeen more, critically injured and unlikely to live," Kreevich said. "I've just had to add one more to the death list, making forty-three."

"Warren Hargrove?"

"Not yet, but the hospital isn't giving him much chance. It seems that Elissa Hargrove had an understudy, a young actress named Betsy Hopkins. She was also backstage when the bomb went off."

"Identified by—?"

"Hell, man, there aren't five people who have been legally identified so far. The count we've made is not from pieces of bodies or the remnants of IDs, like wallets or jewelry. What we have is a list of people we know had to be backstage before the performance was about to begin. People out front who were hurt are more in one piece, buried and crushed, but not blown apart. It was the Hopkins girl's job to report in before each performance—just in case. When Elissa Hargrove was clearly ready to go on, Ms.

32

Hopkins could take off. Her young man was waiting for her to come out of the theater when it blew up. That's how we know she was there. She never showed."

"You said I could help," Quist reminded his friend.

"We have a mass of backtracking to do on dozens of people," Kreevich said. "You and Lydia have a head start in the case of Elissa Hargrove and probably her father. If I knew you were working on her case history, her friends, her enemies, it would free me to tackle Duke Maxwell's story, Mike Naylor's, anyone else's who may emerge as important."

"Pat Walsh probably has a great deal more on Elissa than I have," Quist said.

"But I trust you, friend," Kreevich said. "Use Walsh if you can, but if you'll do it, you're my man."

"I'll use my own people and have a go at it," Quist said. "But we'll need to be authorized to ask questions, examine documents, check accounts—whatever. Without that kind of official help we'll still just be guessing."

"You want the keys to the city, you've got them," Kreevich said.

Lydia arrived shortly after that with the file on Elissa Hargrove. A quick glance at it didn't make Kreevich happy.

"This is the history of her career in films, by and large," he said. "Who her leading men were, who her directors were, bits of gossip, Pat Walsh's articles on her. Any good movie fan would know all this by heart. We have to dig deeper than this, Julian."

"I know," Quist said. "I'll still give it a whirl if you want."

"I want," Kreevich said.

Leaving the interrogation room for the Benson's lobby was like walking into Dante's inferno, with the damned screaming for a hearing. Reporters and TV camera people wanted questions answered by Lieutenant Kreevich and

Captain Stewart. Neither of the police officers in charge had been willing to make any sort of official statement so far.

The list of the dead was mounting. Some of the injured in the audience had been hurried off to nearby hospitals, where they had died. A list of "maybes" was being compiled, people who had friends who thought they had intended to see this night's preview performance of *Undertow*. Then there were the people who "could have been" there, who had announced an intention to go to a preview performance and might have chosen tonight.

The tall, blond, Julian Quist and his lovely lady, Lydia Morton, were instant targets for the reporters who couldn't get to the men in charge. Quist, known to be a friend of Lieutenant Kreevich's, his firm promoting Elissa Hargrove's career, having spent more than an hour in the interrogation room, had to be a source of something real. He and Lydia were literally hemmed in by a crowd of newsmen with no chance of escape available to them. There were no answers to most of the questions fired at them. Did they think the Hargroves had been the main target? Did they know of personal enemies Elissa and her father might have who could be responsible for this holocaust?

"There just hasn't been time to come up with a sensible guess," Quist kept repeating.

There must be some guesses he could make.

"Not yet. It may have nothing to do with the Hargroves at all. A lot of people had died tonight who had no connection with why it was done."

A burly uniformed cop worked his way through the crowd to Quist. "One of the assistant commissioners wants to talk to you, Mr. Quist."

The cop wedged a path through the disappointed reporters toward a door that was marked MANAGER. In the office the "assistant commissioner" turned out to be a happy surprise. Waiting for them was Dan Garvey, Quist's closest friend and one of the associates in Quist's firm. Garvey, dark, intense, powerfully built, was a former professional football star. His knowledge of, and friendships in, the world of sports made him invaluable in many of the promotions that Quist's firm handled.

"Bill Tabor was a linebacker on the old team," Garvey said, indicating the cop who had rescued Quist and Lydia. "Thanks, Bill."

"My pleasure," the cop said and left the three friends alone.

"And thank you, Dan," Quist said. "Those vultures out there wouldn't give us an inch."

"I figured you'd be here," Garvey said. "It's hell over there across the street. I know it must have hit you pretty hard when you heard about it."

Quist took a handkerchief out of his breast pocket and blotted at his face with it. The perspiration felt cold. "It's hard to believe that it's happened," he said. "So far it's just names and numbers, statistics. Get away from this, and the full impact of it will hit home, I guess."

"I've got something for you," Garvey said, "but it requires an agreement from you before I tell you what it is."

"Agreement?"

"You have to promise not to talk to Kreevich or Stewart or anyone else in authority until you've talked to someone I want you to see."

"Kreevich is my friend. I've agreed to help him."

"Then I can't tell you what I've got," Garvey said, his voice harsh. "I wouldn't ask you to hold out unless I thought it was the right thing for you to do."

"Come on, Dan! What kind of double-talk—?"

"Have I ever played any silly games with you, Julian?"

"No, but—"

"There's someone who needs to talk to you," Garvey said.

"When I tell you who it is, you will want to run to Kreevich. You have to promise me you won't go to Kreevich until after you've talked to the person."

Lydia's hand tightened on Quist's arm. "I'll promise, if it matters," she said.

"Dan, I'll have to use my own judgement," Quist said. "If it's something I think Kreevich should have, I'll go to him."

"But not till after you've talked to the person who has something to hide from him. Hear what it is. Then use your own judgement. But not before you've listened."

"When can I talk to this person?"

"Ten minutes after we can get away from here," Garvey said.

"Okay, I'll go that far," Quist said.

"Buckle your seat belts," Garvey said. A little nerve twitched at the corner of his mouth. "Elissa wasn't in the Quatermayne when it blew up."

Quist took one quick step to his friend and grabbed him by the shoulders. "Who told you that?"

"Elissa," Garvey said.

Quist shook his head, like a fighter trying to clear his head from a dazing punch.

"When you get home and check the answering service on your phone, you'll find that earlier in the evening someone called you every ten minutes asking you to call a number. That someone was Elissa. She'd heard the news, just as you and I did, on a radio or TV. She needed help, and you were the only person she knew of who could give it to her. Finally, she took a chance and called me."

"But why—?"

"She has to tell you, and you've promised not to pass this along till she does."

"Where is she?"

"My apartment." Garvey's smile was tight. "Can you walk yet?"

3

"Walking" was not a joke. Garvey's linebacker cop got them out a rear entrance of the hotel, but in the turmoil still existing out on the street, there was no way to find a taxi to take them anywhere. It was four long crosstown blocks to Garvey's apartment on Lexington Avenue.

"I should think Elissa would want to be with her father," Lydia said, when they were out of the crowds and headed east.

"Friend of mine is on the emergency staff at Bellevue," Garvey said. "That's where they took Warren Hargrove. I checked for Elissa. An hour ago he was still alive, but not conscious, not likely to make it. And I think Elissa is praying that he doesn't make it."

"Why?" Quist asked.

"If he makes it, it's a hundred-to-one, he'll be a vegetable," Garvey said. "Head smashed, brain damage, hopeless."

"So much for wealth and power when you need it," Quist said.

Garvey's apartment on Lexington Avenue was familiar to both Quist and Lydia. Quist had once jokingly called it the "Trophy Room." There were pictures of Garvey's high school, college, and professional football teams, on all of which he had been a star running back, as well as auto-graphed photographs of famous athletes who had been Gar-vey's friends along the way. There was a glass case contain-ing cups and medals and an autographed football Dan had carried over the goal line in a Rose Bowl game. There was nothing to suggest that any woman had ever had anything to do with decorating the place.

Garvey opened the door with his own key and stepped in. "Elissa!" he called out. "Friends!"

She came out of the bedroom, moving almost like a sleepwalker, her lovely face ravaged by tears.

"Julian!" It was a hoarse whisper. And then she was in his arms, her whole body shaking.

Quist didn't say anything, just held her close, waiting for the shaking and trembling to pass. In the background Lydia was asking Dan if he had the makings of coffee in his kitchenette. After a moment Quist moved the weeping actress over to the sofa in front of Garvey's fireplace, eased her down, and sat beside her, holding both her ice-cold hands in his.

"I don't have to tell you what a marvelous surprise it is to find you alive and well and all in one piece," he said.

She lifted her tear-streaked face. "Not quite all in one piece," she said, still in that strange hoarse whisper she had used to greet him. She lifted her hand and touched her throat with unsteady fingers. "Laryngitis," she said. "It saved my life."

"Take your time," Quist said.

"This morning—or is it yesterday morning now—I—I woke up with this. No voice. A doctor the stage manager recommended gave me some kind of inhaler to use and medication. He thought, by evening, I should have re-covered enough to go on stage. I rested all day, took the medicine, used the inhaler, and did some vocal exercises I'd learned from my voice teacher. I—I'd never had laryn-gitis before, so I expected some kind of miracle."

"It didn't happen?"

Elissa shook her head. "I went to the theater at six-thirty, which is the time I'm supposed to check in. Everything normal—except me. I—I kept trying to get myself to make some usable sounds. Nothing but this croaking whisper. So, at about seven-thirty, I sent for Betsy Hopkins, my understudy, who was standing by and told her she'd have to go on for me. If it had been a regular performance, it would have involved a decision by the management—refunds to people in the audience, perhaps no show. But a preview? It wasn't a matter of life and death." She gave a choking, bitter little laughing sound. "What am I saying? It was a matter of life and death! I—I went back to my apartment, and poor, dear Betsy died in my place."

She couldn't go on for a moment. Finally Quist prompted her. "You left the theater?"

She nodded. "Went back to my apartment and went to bed. I think you know I've sublet a place only a couple of blocks from the Quatermayne. I tried to forget my aches and pains and get some rest. I was in bed when I heard the explosion and then the sirens of police cars and ambulances. I was curious, because it all sounded like something out of the ordinary, so I switched on the radio on the bedside table. And there it was—the Quatermayne had been blown to bits, and I—I and my father—were among the dead or near dead."

"You'd known your father was in the theater?"

"No! Maybe you won't understand, Julian. Dad and I are so very close. I knew he'd come to one of the preview performances, but he wouldn't tell me in advance. Knowing he was there might interfere with my concentration, do something to my nerves! Oh, I have nerves at every performance, even if a play has run six months. Stage fright, they call it."

"You know what the report is on your father?"

She lifted her hands and covered her face with them. A

long, shuddering sigh escaped between her fingers. "Dan Garvey called the hospital for me. They don't think he's going to make it. If he does—they say dreadful things."

"You know how important it is for the police to know that you're alive," Quist said, after another brief silence. "You may be able to give them help they badly need. Hundreds of thousands of your film fans will be delighted to know that you weren't in that disaster. Why are you asking us to keep it a secret?"

She lowered her hands and looked straight at him. "Because I want to go on living," she said.

"Sounds like a reasonable goal, don't you think, Julian?" Garvey asked. He'd drifted back from the kitchenette, where Lydia was making coffee.

"The best way to be certain would be to have the strongest possible defenses. Kreevich and the cops would be miles ahead of you or me, Dan," Quist said.

"We have one thing on them," Garvey said. "We can keep a secret."

Quist made an impatient gesture. "You two have already discussed this," he said. "Hadn't you better let me in on your thinking, starting at square one?"

"Shall I start it off for him, Lissa?" Garvey asked. "Save your voice for his questions."

Cutting off the first letter of her name suggested to Quist that Dan hadn't wasted any time getting on an intimate footing with the lady. She had needed that, he thought. She nodded to Garvey who, to coin a cliché, took the ball.

"To begin with, Lissa thinks the attack was aimed at her and, possibly, her father," Garvey said.

"Why?" Quist interrupted. "Duke Maxwell had the most to lose by the kind of attack it was, not just his life, his valuable property. Mike Naylor had violent enemies. There are other people who haven't surfaced yet on the casualty list."

"Lissa thinks—"

"It won't do, Dan," Elissa said. "He's got to hear it from me—if he can stand this." She reached up to touch her throat, an apology for the rasping whisper.

Lydia had come from the kitchenette with something in a water glass. "This may help," she said. "Old-fashioned remedy—honey and lemon juice." She smiled at Elissa. "Be a good girl and swallow slowly."

Elissa nodded her thanks and sipped from the glass. After a moment she turned back to Quist. "Can you stand hearing it from me, Julian? It will save you some questions."

"Please," he said.

"I spent a lot of my growing-up time in the Middle East," she said. "Lebanon, Israel, Egypt, Syria, Iran, and Libya. Mass violence was an everyday thing, like cornflakes for breakfast. Bombs thrown in busses, public gathering places, military installations—like our marines last year. Always many people killed, and not always as it was supposed to appear, just a violence against a particular country, a special group. Often one special person was the target—a political figure, an enemy diplomat, a counterrevolutionary. My father calls it 'the Kamikaze syndrome.' The bomber dies in his own act of destruction—like the man who drove an explosives-loaded truck into our marine barracks. What happened at the Quatermayne has all the earmarks of that kind of pattern. Obscure the real motive by making the violence cover a wide area. The police think it may have been aimed at the Hargroves, thanks to Pat Walsh's press campaign against us; they think it may have been aimed at Duke Maxwell, who was buddy-buddy with underworld people; or at Mike Naylor, who was a labor racketeer. There won't be one shred of solid evidence to prove any one of those theories."

"Not yet, anyway," Quist said. "But you think you know it was aimed at you?"

"If you were driving somewhere in your car with a

friend," Elissa said, "and someone fired a shot at you that killed your friend, the police would go looking for someone who wanted to get that friend. But you might know, secretly, that the shot was meant for you and missed. That's the way it was at the Quatermayne."

"You were meant to die, only they missed?"

She nodded and took another sip of Lydia's potion.

"So, you tell that to the police, and they go looking for your killer or killers," Quist said.

"There's no way on earth the police, even your good friend Lieutenant Kreevich, could keep my being alive a secret. The minute cops are out investigating, here or in the Middle East, or in Europe, someone would let it slip. Then I am a target again."

"But with police protection," Quist said.

Elissa leaned forward. "If I am the target, then there will be not just one killer but an army of them out to get me. Hide me away somewhere, and they will blow up the hiding place, killing me and the police protecting me."

"So, keep your being alive a secret, you still have to hide," Quist said. "You can't walk down the hall without being recognized."

"Not if I don't want to be recognized. Makeup, disguise are simple enough. And if my enemies think they succeeded, Julian, they'll be off guard."

"Against what? No one will have anything to go on, nothing that will threaten them."

"That's where you come in," Elissa said.

"I'm all ears," Quist said.

"You have been engaged to protect me against the kind of slander Pat Walsh and others have been aiming at me. You could have all kinds of valuable information from me that would help the police."

"But I don't. Kreevich already has my file on you, which isn't much more than a history of your professional career."

"I could have made tapes for you that would give you important facts," Elissa said.

"But you haven't."

"I could and will. You could remember that I promised to make them, and they turn up in the mail for you. They will start your friend Kreevich on the right track. Meanwhile, an eighty-year-old hag wanders around town, searching the garbage pails for something to eat. Not Elissa Hargrove. Impossible! She was killed in the Quatermayne bombing."

Quist leaned back against the couch. It was an insane idea, and yet—and yet . . .

"She stays safe, you feed Kreevich what she has," Garvey said. "You haven't betrayed him, and you help make sure that she stays alive. She can't tell him anymore than she will tape for you, which you will pass on to him."

Quist stood up, walked to the far end of the room and back. He stopped in front of Elissa.

"I'll go a short way with this," he said. "You want to talk into a tape machine, I'll listen to what you produce. If it's enough to give Kreevich something solid, I may go along with you for a while."

"I still want to stay alive, Julian!"

"I want that, too, love," he said. "But I've got to be sure this is the right way."

"Tape machine coming up," Garvey said.

Turning Elissa loose on Garvey's tape machine didn't make much sense, Quist knew. He should sit with the woman, be able to question her when she came up with something that wasn't clear. He should, he very well knew, be bundling her into a cab and taking her to Kreevich at the Benson Hotel. The excuse for going ahead with the taping, with delaying a moment of truth with Kreevich, was a bone-aching fatigue. He had spent most of the previous day at the home of a client in the country, planning the promotion of a big sales campaign. On the way home, there had been the radio account of the tragedy at the Quatermayne, hours of tension since then.

"I don't know, if someone suddenly asked me my name, whether I could answer," he said to Lydia. They were in a taxi, going from Dan Garvey's apartment to their own on Beekman Place. "Couple of hours sleep, and I may be able to make sense out of whatever Elissa's story is."

"You may be sorry later that you're holding out on Mark," Lydia said.

"I may," Quist said. "But I'd be sorrier still if something happened to Elissa before we can set up the proper protection for her." He stirred restlessly as the cab stopped for a red light. "Elissa hinted that her enemies are in the Middle East, with millions in oil money to spend. A leak could be bought, right in Kreevich's office. If nobody knows, nobody gets to know."

It seemed to Quist that he had only just put his head down on the pillow when his bedside telephone rang. Daylight was streaming through the open windows across the room. He had to have slept for three or four hours.

The caller was Dan Garvey. His voice sounded harsh. "I have a tape for you, Julian," he said. "I thought I'd bring it over—if you're willing and able."

"Come," Quist said.

"Things are pretty hairy here. I hate to leave Lissa alone, but I don't want to trust this to a messenger."

"Hairy?"

"I just checked with the hospital for Lissa," Garvey said. "Warren Hargrove died about a half an hour ago. Could be a blessing, but from where Lissa sits—a father is a father."

"He could probably have told us ten times more than Elissa can," Quist said.

"You may be surprised," Garvey said. "I'm on my way."

* * *

Garvey brought the tape. Quist was up and having freshly made coffee when he arrived.

"Like the earth opened up and swallowed her," Garvey said. He had brought his own tape machine to be sure there were no problems in playing the tape. He crossed his fingers. "She and her old man must have been close as that. She reacts more like losing a lover than a parent. I try to tell her it is probably for the best. He would never have been himself again. It doesn't help."

"I can imagine."

"I'm going back to her. She shouldn't be alone. You and Lydia and I are the only people she can be with without blowing her secret."

"You've heard this tape?" Quist asked.

"I was with her while she made it," Garvey said. "It may curl your hair just a little."

Lydia joined Quist when he put the tape in the machine and was ready to listen. Elissa's voice was still the husky whisper they'd last heard, but it came through quite clearly on the sensitive tape. The machine made a whirring noise as the tape started to wind, and there she was.

"Mr. Quist—I thought of trying to make this tape sound as if it had been made before tonight, so that your friend, Lieutenant Kreevich, could hear it and not know that I was still alive. It seemed too difficult and would have involved endless phony elaborations. So, here it is—and my life is in your hands.

"It is a long history of duplicity, but patriotic duplicity, Mr. Quist. As you know, my father and I have spent a lot of my lifetime in the Middle East. My father is concerned with oil, enormous quantities that are needed in his business. He has been prepared to deal with anyone who had it to sell, friend or foe. So is our government, by the way. Dad has maintained a friendly footing with friendly leaders who changed sides from time to time. There was the Shah of Iran, and then Khomeini; there have been changing top men in Egypt, and Syria, and Libya, and Lebanon. I had a role in this as I grew up and was lucky enough to make a reputation for myself as a film star. That role was to appear sympathetic to those men who controlled oil. What I really thought or think hasn't mattered. I had a part to play. Warren Hargrove's daughter had different opinions than most conservative people in the West and was able to make her views public because of her position as a film star. I said what I was instructed to say, Mr. Quist, by my father. I would have said whatever he wanted me to say, even if I disagreed. Did I disagree? Yes, eventually, and I told my father so. He was selling weapons and technology to the enemy, just to gain access to their oil supplies.

"That was when my father told me the truth. It's a truth, Mr. Quist, that you won't be able to prove unless my father is willing to help you—when he's back on his feet. My father has been working for the CIA all these years. Yes, he has sold weapons and high technology to the enemy, all just a little outdated. A list of every single item has been passed on to the CIA so that our people have always been ready to overmatch the enemy with more modern, more efficient equipment. If this ever got to be known, we were in big trouble. The Arabs, who thought my father was their friend, would destroy him. My father said: 'I may be buried under the Washington monument as a national hero, but I don't care to be dead, Lissy.' I'd been a heroine without knowing it! So you see, Mr. Quist, what Pat Walsh has been writing about us has been true, without coming close to guessing at the real truth.

"I can see your eyes lighting up. All you have to do is go to the CIA, get them to admit what's been going on, and everybody in the Western world will be out to defend us, pin medals on us. The only trouble with that, Julian, is the CIA will deny it until they are blue in the face. To admit it would be to reveal a whole network of counterespionage. My father and I would undoubtedly pay with our lives, along with dozens of other undercover agents, some real, some just guessed at by the enemy. So you know, and it isn't going to do you any good to know.

"But the enemy are not fools, Julian. They have the means to buy treachery—oil millions. Someone in the know had a price. That brings us to last night. A few days ago my father got a warning. He must provide the enemy with first-rate weapons, the most modern technology, or he would suffer a loss he would find hard to endure. The game was up, it seemed. My father reached his contacts and told them it would take time for him to meet their demands. They told him they would give him no time. Two days— and the Quatermayne. I—I was the loss my father would find hard to endure. Can I name who is responsible, who bought the bombers, who set it up? I can name a dozen groups who might have. Will we start World War Three to punish them? I doubt it."

The tape ran blank for a moment, and then Elissa's voice came back, shaken and out of control.

"Oh God, Julian, Dan has just called the hospital, and Dad is gone. Without him there is a tangle here you'll never be able to put together. I don't know if I care anymore. There's nothing to care about."

There was no more on the tape.

By ten o'clock that morning, the Quatermayne story was everywhere—all over the world. Garvey, on his way home from delivering the tape to Quist, had picked up the newspapers. Black headlines announced the story in all its gruesome details. Elissa and three other famous actors were dead; Warren Hargrove, the star's millionaire industrialist father, was dead; Duke Maxwell, the colorful sports and theatrical promotor, had been blown to bits on his own stage in his own theater; Mike Naylor, prominent labor leader, had been in the very center of the death-dealing blast; a well-known writer and historian and his wife had been crushed to death in the audience area under the collapsing cement and steel of the theater's roof. There was a long list of other names, "not yet complete" according to the police, who had died—carpenters, electricians, stagehands, wardrobe women, dressers, a stage doorman, an usher who had brought an as yet unexplained message to Duke Maxwell that had taken him backstage just before the blast. Most of those who had been killed under the collapsing roof had had some kind of decipherable identification. The names would mean something to grieving families and friends, but all of them were strangers to Garvey.

Back in the apartment, he switched on the radio. Pat Walsh was on somebody's talk show, having himself a field day. He had been an eyewitness to the horror, had his own private theory that the Hargroves had been the target of a terrorist group. He suggested, slyly, that eventually things might be revealed about Warren Hargrove that might shock the American public. Garvey wondered, angrily, if Walsh would have risked that kind of statement if he'd known Elissa was alive. With her dead, there'd be no one to bring a libel suit. Alive, she just might take him to the cleaners.

Today she wasn't in shape to care whether school kept or not. He had looked into the bedroom when he got back from Quist's. She was lying there, arms above her head, staring at the ceiling, as if she thought some kind of healing vision might suddenly appear there. He'd asked if he could get her anything. She had just closed her eyes and turned her head, slightly, away from him. There are times when comforting conversation is worse than nothing. Garvey guessed this was one of those times and left her to deal with her grief in private.

About eleven o'clock the front door buzzer sounded. Garvey spoke into the intercom phone and heard Julian's voice. He pressed the button that released the front-door lock down a flight. A moment later there was a knock on Garvey's door. Garvey opened it. Julian Quist was there, but not alone. With him was Lieutenant Mark Kreevich of Manhattan Homicide.

Anger surged up in Garvey. "You son-of-a-bitch!" he said to his friend.

"Sorry," Quist said, "but I had to use my own judgement. Mark doesn't know yet why he's here."

"I guess I ought to have my head examined," Kreevich said. "In the middle of the most complex murder investigation in the history of the city, I let Julian persuade me that, if I'd come here with him, he could present me with some kind of vital information. If I told the commissioner that I dropped everything just because I trust a man, he'd have my badge."

"And be right!" Garvey said. "I trusted him, too."

"In any case there isn't time to play word Ping-Pong," Kreevich said. He looked at Quist. "Can we bring whatever it is out on the table, Julian?"

The door at the far end of the room opened, and Elissa stood there, tall, golden, pale, beautiful. Kreevich reached out a hand to the door jamb, needing to steady himself.

"Miss Hargrove?"

Elissa nodded. She was focused on Quist. "I'm sorry you didn't see fit to keep your word, Julian. But perhaps it doesn't matter anymore. I'm no longer quite so concerned with staying alive."

"Good Lord, woman, do you realize they're saying prayers for you all over the country, all over the world?" Kreevich asked.

"So you might as well come in. The ball game seems to be over," Garvey said.

Quist walked into the room. He was carrying Garvey's tape machine, and he put it down on the center table. "I'm sorry I've turned out to be a creep," he said to Elissa. "However you feel about living, I care very much that you do." He turned to Kreevich and quickly explained how Elissa had managed to escape the bombing, turned to him for help, and failing to find him, had gone to Garvey.

"Bypassing the people who needed the truth—the police," Kreevich said.

"Elissa and Dan felt there was no way the police could be told without the word getting out that she was alive. Elissa felt she would still be a target for murder. They asked me to promise not to pass the word along to you. I promised, but I changed my mind." He turned to the table and opened the case that held the tape machine. "Elissa made this tape for me after I'd promised. I changed my mind after I'd heard it."

Kreevich turned to the girl. "You want me to hear this, Miss Hargrove? There's nothing that says you have to let it be played for me. If you do, it will become a part of the case."

"With my father dead, nothing matters," Elissa said.

Quist put the tape in place and pressed the "play" button. The whole story of Warren Hargrove's involvements in the Middle East, Elissa's cooperation, the connection with the CIA, and the final threat two days ago from an unnamed enemy, was revealed for Kreevich. The detective turned away when the final little segment indicating that Elissa knew about her father began—and finished. There was a long silence in the room, and finally Quist spoke to Elissa.

"It may not matter to you to know why I broke my promise and brought Mark into the picture," he said, "but I'd like to tell you."

She turned her back to him, and he could see the shaking in her shoulders.

"When I'd heard the tape," Quist went on, "I knew there was no way on earth that Dan and I, two ordinary citizens, could protect you against the people you described. You told me that you wanted to stay alive, and I cared very much. I knew that, if he heard the truth, Mark would have access to the means, the men, who might keep you safe. I knew that if he heard all the facts, just as I'd heard them, he could make an intelligent judgement as to whether letting the public know that you were alive, or keeping it a secret, was the safest thing for you. I didn't tell him till he got here and could see you and listen. I want you safe, love."

Kreevich moved over to stand directly behind Elissa. "I think Julian did the right thing for you, Miss Hargrove," he said. "Just what the next step is has to be thought about, there's so much I still don't know. But, believe me, every single resource at my disposal will be used to protect you."

"So call the newspapers and make her a target!" Garvey said, in an angry voice.

"Come on, Dan, grow up!" Kreevich said.

"Sorry, master!" Garvey said.

"I know it's difficult for you to talk, Miss Hargrove, having gotten the news about your father. But talk we must, if I'm to be of any help at all."

Elissa turned around, using a tissue to blot at the tears that had stained her cheeks. "I think I believe, Julian, that you did what you thought was best for me. I don't know if you were right or not, but I don't have any choice but to go along with it."

"She's just throwing in the towel," Garvey said, still angry. "She was safe before I made the mistake of bringing Julian into the picture. Dead, she was safe. Let the truth out, and the bastards who want to get her can hire killers to come at her from all over the world. They have that kind of money, that kind of reach and power."

"You mention a list of your father's potential enemies on the tape, Miss Hargrove," Kreevich said.

"I can give you a list of the people he sold weapons to, and you can be sure not one of them was within thousands of miles of the Quatermayne last night," Elissa said.

"Like the attack on the marines in Beirut," Garvey said. "One kamikaze kook drives a truck loaded with explosives into the marine post, blows it up, kills himself—and two hundred and fifty marines. The real villain is sitting at home in his palace, or whatever, sipping a glass of wine and rejoicing in the news. You're going to be damned lucky, Mark, to connect a mangled corpse in the Quatermayne to a high-up customer of Warren Hargrove's in the Middle East."

"I don't need your help, Dan, to point out the difficulties in this case," Kreevich said. He turned to Elissa. "I'd like that list from you before I leave, Miss Hargrove, but meanwhile there are some things that bug me. You say that some of your father's 'customers' had discovered he was selling them outdated weapons. They warned him that he must provide them with up-to-date equipment or suffer a loss he would find hard to endure. Meaning you, you think?"

Elissa nodded.

"But they wouldn't give him time? Even a madman would have to know he couldn't deliver overnight. They *had* to give him time if what they really wanted was modern weapons. Two days? No way could he meet their demands in two days. Weapons have to be loaded, transported over thousands of miles of ocean. Killing you couldn't speed up the process."

Elissa didn't respond.

"And killing your father has put an end to the whole deal," Kreevich said.

"They had no way of knowing he would be there," Elissa said. "I didn't know myself that he was coming." She went into the explanation of how her father didn't tell her in advance that he was going to attend a performance—nerves, stage fright.

"That doesn't mean he might not have told someone else he intended to be there last night, as long as it didn't get back to you," Kreevich said.

"I suppose," Elissa said. "It would have to have been just the wrong person, wouldn't it? Someone who would report to the bomber that this was the night Dad would be there."

"And so that's the signal to set off the bombs?" Kreevich shook his head. "Men with millions of dollars to spend on arming their country for a war would go to such lengths for revenge?"

"A message to anyone else who was dealing with them," Garvey suggested.

"There were three bombs set in the theater," Kreevich said, "one back of the light board, one backstage, and one in the ceiling out over the front row of seats in the audience area. They had to have been set in place at some time when the theater was relatively deserted. Captain Stewart is certain that the thing that set them off was a connection behind the light board. That connection had to have been made *after* the board was tested at six forty-five. Someone in the theater. A stranger would have been noticed."

"But nobody left alive who can report having seen a stranger," Quist said.

"Did you see anyone wandering around, Miss Hargrove, who didn't belong there?" Kreevich asked.

"I didn't see anyone wandering anywhere," Elissa said. "I had this thing, this laryngitis. I went straight to my dressing room when I got to the theater. My dresser Sally Bond was there. Poor, dear Sally!" Elissa's voice broke, but she got it back in control. "I knew the chances were I couldn't go on. I sent for the stage manager and told him. Betsy Hopkins, my understudy, was notified and came to my dressing room. Finally I had to decide. I couldn't make it. I slipped out the stage door, went back to my apartment. When I got there, I turned on the radio—or the TV, I don't remember which—and there was the bombing. I tried to reach Julian and eventually got Dan. That was my evening, Lieutenant."

Kreevich nodded, almost as though he hadn't been listening. "There are two people who got lucky last night, and one who got very unlucky."

"You've got dozens of dead, and only one person got unlucky?"

Kreevich was still a man thinking out loud. "You, Miss Hargrove, developed a laryngitis, which kept you from being where you would otherwise have been. Phil Guardino, the second electrician, was sent across the street by Mike Naylor to get some coffee. Otherwise he would have been standing right by the bomb that exploded behind the light board. You two were the lucky ones."

"And your particular unlucky one?" Quist asked.

"Duke Maxwell," Kreevich said. "According to Fred Vail, Duke was out in the lobby greeting friends and guests who were coming to the preview. Normally, he would have stayed there, but an usher brought him a message that took him backstage. Can you make a guess at what that message was, Miss Hargrove?"

"I've guessed and guessed at that," Elissa said. "It could have been me."

"Someone sent him a message that you weren't going to be able to go on?"

"It's possible—logical," Elissa said. "Someone would have to inform the audience that I wasn't going to appear, offer an apology, refunds if people wanted them."

"And Duke Maxwell would have been the one to do that?" Kreevich asked. "Not one of the actors or the stage manager?"

"Duke, at any rate, would have had to decide who was going to make the announcement," Elissa said. "I think he'd have wanted to make it himself. There was a special audience, a big group of people in the sports world who were Duke's friends."

"So he makes the decision to make the announcement. What then?"

Elissa looked as if the words she spoke gave her actual pain. "They would have lowered the house lights, Duke would have stepped out between the center break in the curtain—"

"And when they lowered the lights, the world blew up," Garvey said.

"That still doesn't make Duke the target," Quist said. "No one could have foreseen Elissa's problem in the late afternoon when the bombs must have been put in place."

Kreevich nodded. "He would have been expected to be in the lobby, acting as host for the evening."

"From where he would see his property destroyed, his people butchered," Garvey said.

"You played for him didn't you, Dan, on his football team?" Kreevich asked. "You knew him, personally?"

"About seven years' worth," Garvey said. "Sure I knew him. He paid me a handsome salary. I was his golden boy, you could say. He had nothing to do with the play on the field, but he hired the people who did. After a big win, he would throw parties; he liked to show off his stars. I was expected to be present, to be shown off to Duke's friends."

"Dan was one of the great players of his time," Quist said.

"So, who were Maxwell's friends? Who were his enemies?" Kreevich asked.

"If he had enemies, they are under a rock somewhere," Garvey said. "Duke wasn't cut out to be a loser."

"Until last night," Quist said.

"Unlucky, as Mark said." Garvey managed a bitter smile. "Duke was a man who couldn't imagine dying. He couldn't imagine anything but success. He couldn't understand any figure that had less than six zeros after it. He expected to always win big."

"A three-million-dollar lottery, wasn't it?" Quist asked.

" 'Them that has, gits,' " Garvey said. "He bought a football team, but nothing less than winning the Super Bowl would satisfy him. He decides to produce a play, but nothing less than a star of Lissa's magnitude would satisfy him."

"What enemies under what rocks?" Kreevich persisted, as though he hadn't been listening.

"I didn't mean any particular enemy or any special rock," Garvey said. "I just meant, if somebody tried to cross Duke or get in his way, he'd have been buried alive. Duke had the money and the clout to brush off anyone who got in his way like you or I would brush off a mosquito. Generous to people he liked and could help him get what he wanted in some field of interest. He bought me a Mercedes-Benz once, just for scoring a touchdown against the Raiders. I understand he had half a million bucks bet on that game, so buying me a car wasn't that far out of line."

"Women?" Kreevich asked.

"He attracted them like bees to the honey," Garvey said. "Duke was surrounded by them."

Kreevich turned his head. "You were drawn to him, Miss Hargrove?"

Elissa looked startled. "Are you asking if I had something romantic going with him?" she asked.

"If you did."

"I never laid eyes on the man or heard of him until some months ago," she said, after a moment. "I'm not a sports fan. I don't read the gossip columns—unless they're about me."

"But you went to work for him."

"That was my father's doing."

"He knew Maxwell?"

"Dad was a sports nut," Elissa said. "I think he owned a piece of Maxwell's football team. About the play, Jeb Carleton, the author, brought it to me in Hollywood. He wanted me for the lead and nobody else. Of course I was flattered and delighted. I loved the play. Jeb thought if he had me he'd have no trouble finding a producer. My father suggested his friend Duke Maxwell. Duke had just rebuilt the Quatermayne, and he wanted the right play and the right star to open it with a splash. Dad went to him, and he was instantly ready to do business. He drew up a contract for me that you wouldn't believe; I would agree to stay with the play as long as it ran on Broadway. If I got a film offer in that time, he, Duke, would match it!"

"Like I said, six zeros after a number didn't scare Duke," Garvey said.

"So he bought you, Miss Hargrove," Kreevich said.

"I don't like the sound of that," Elissa said. "Duke bought my talents as an actress, my ability to draw customers in at the box office. He didn't buy me."

"Not for sale, I'd guess," Quist said.

"Thank you, Julian," Elissa said.

"But the man was a man," Garvey said. "He couldn't look at you, Lissa, and not dream some dreams."

"I suppose I've encountered every kind of man-on-the-make there is," Elissa said. "That goes with my world, my career, my special kind of exposure. Duke Maxwell was unique. He, quite literally, apologized to me for not making a play for me. It was as if I had a right to expect it and was entitled to an explanation of why he hadn't suggested a romance."

"I'd like an explanation for that myself," Garvey said, grinning at Elissa. "Duke assumed he was irresistible, so passing up a go for you doesn't make sense."

Perhaps some other time Elissa would have been pleased by what was obviously meant to be a compliment. Still overcome by the loss of her father, flattery did nothing for her. "Duke came to me the first day of rehearsal," she said. "He was all smiles, all charm. He said I shouldn't be puzzled if he didn't seem to be interested in me 'in a man-woman way. I'm a one-at-a-time guy,' he told me. 'A certain girl has me roped and hog-tied at the moment. I look forward to the day when I get unhooked and we can talk about something other than your play and the weather.' I asked him who the lucky lady was."

"And—?" Kreevich asked.

"Sandra Cleaves. She's a nightclub singer."

"She's singing at Marty's Mansion in the East Sixties," Quist said. "A first-class talent. Duke must have had to fight off an army that's also interested in her."

"Rough night and day for her," Kreevich said. "She's been on to us a half dozen times, hoping against hope, I guess, that there was some mistake about Duke."

"There must be scores of other people hoping there must be 'some mistake' about someone they cared for," Quist said.

"Let's get back to you, Miss Hargrove," Kreevich said. "This list of names you're going to give me. Does anyone in particular stand out as the one most likely to want to do in your father and you?"

Elissa shook her head, slowly. "A lot of those men in the Middle East who dealt with my father are like villains in some romantic melodrama," she said. "They're all prepared to do what they do in a spectacular fashion. But they can also be silent, quiet, deadly. If they knew I'd escaped, they could send someone to cut my throat while I was asleep." She lowered her head, looking exhausted. "A little while ago that's what frightened me. Now it doesn't matter much."

"It matters to me, whether or not it matters to you, Miss Hargrove," Kreevich said. "It's my job to keep you safe— and every other citizen in this town! Whether or not to let the public know that you escaped the bombing at the theater—?" He looked impatient with his uncertainty.

"It's a situation you can't put back in place, Mark, once you let the cat out of the bag," Quist said. "I can see advantages both ways."

"Show me any place where there's an advantage in this case and I'll pin a medal on you," Kreevich said.

Quist shrugged his shoulders. "Let it stand the way it is—Elissa died in the bombing—and it will be relatively simple to keep her safe."

"Because nobody will be looking for her?"

"Right. But let it be known that she escaped, and maybe someone will come looking. If you're ready, you grab him."

"Use Miss Hargrove as bait, in other words?" Kreevich asked.

"Look, she's alive and well and here in this room," Garvey said angrily. "She's not some chess piece in a game!"

"I can keep you alive for a while, either way, Miss Hargrove," Kreevich said. "Not forever, though. These people want to get you badly enough, they can just wait until somebody relaxes for a few minutes—which will happen, sooner or later."

"You pays your money and you takes your choice," Quist said.

"I'd like time to prepare something pretty thorough in the way of protection," Kreevich said. "You'd have to play along, Miss Hargrove. Poke your nose out the door, somebody sees you, and the whole world will know you're alive in ten seconds!"

"It doesn't matter very much anymore," Elissa said, in the hoarse whisper that kept any emotion out of her words.

"It doesn't matter to you whether the people who murdered your father get what's coming to them?" Quist asked.

She turned to look at him, her blue eyes suddenly cold as winter ice. "It matters!" she said. "It matters, matters, matters!" She turned to Kreevich. "Where do you want to hide me, Lieutenant."

"I'd like not to risk moving you, if Dan agrees," Kreevich said.

"Of course, I agree," Garvey said.

"I'll post a man in the first floor entrance, another up

here in the hall outside. It will probably take me half an hour, maybe an hour, to get the right two men assigned to me."

"I'll stay with her. She'll be safe," Garvey said.

"You go along, Miss Hargrove?" Kreevich asked.

Elissa nodded.

"Use the time while we're getting ready to make me that list of names," Kreevich said.

While Kreevich used the phone to call headquarters and ask for two specific detectives to be assigned to him and sent to Garvey's apartment, Elissa Hargrove sat at Garvey's desk, making her list of names for the detective. When Kreevich was finished on the phone, he beckoned to Quist, and the two men went out into the small vestibule, out of earshot of the others.

"More chiefs than Indians on this case just now," Kreevich said. "If there is any way to screw things up, the boys at the top will figure it out."

"Chiefs?" Quist asked him.

"The CIA is in the picture. From what Miss Hargrove's told us, we can guess why. The FBI is on the job. Did I tell you that among the people killed in the theater audience was Joey Torio, there with some girl friend. Both crushed to death under a block of cement."

"Who is Joey Torio?"

"Son of Benito Torio, godfather to the mobs in this area. The FBI thinks we may be involved in some kind of gang war—and see a chance to reap some glory for themselves if they're right. Whoever solves this case, because of the celebrities involved, can ask for just about anything and get it. The DA's office has a special investigator on the job. The mayor is demanding results. Down the line there is Captain Stewart and me, just a couple of day laborers who'll have to do the job."

"You're satisfied with keeping the news about Elissa under your hat?" Quist asked.

"Can give us a little elbow room," Kreevich said. "Spill it, and the news people from all over the world will bury us alive. No way to do anything else but fight them off. This way we ward them off, and we have a better chance of protecting Elissa—if she's in danger."

"If?"

"If the word gets out that she survived the bombing, then, if somebody was out to get her, they'll try again. Keep her buried, and no one will come gunning for her. They'll think they have won."

"So you think she was the target—she, and perhaps her father?"

"Julian, I haven't the faintest idea at the moment. I haven't one single fact that makes anything certain."

"What Elissa gave us on that tape?"

"That thousands of miles away there are some big-shot terrorists who might have had it in for her and her old man? What I have to find, friend, is the man or men, right here, who set those bombs and triggered them for the payoff. If they were hired by terrorists thousands of miles away, that's up to the State Department, the CIA, the Pentagon, or the president himself. My chances are pretty damn slim. There seems not to be a single living witness who saw anything, who can tell me anything."

"There is, of course, somebody alive who knows."

"Sure. The guy who did it, and the guy who hired him. The guy who did it is probably headed for home, wherever that is, a rich man. The guy who hired him got what he paid for."

"Not if he was after Elissa."

"Which is why I'm going along with this cover-up. Which brings me to you, chum. I want you to do what you'd do if you didn't know what you know. You had things planned for her, appearances, benefits, all to make her look like a nice, clean-cut, patriotic American girl. You have to cancel those things, notify people, answer questions, express your shock and grief."

"Lydia knows, of course," Quist said.

"Lydia will play it exactly the way you tell her to," Kreevich said. "Go to your office, Julian. Go through the routines you'd go through if you didn't know the truth. Keep the press happy."

It made sense. Quist called his apartment to alert Lydia, but there was no answer. That puzzled him for a moment. They had an automatic answering service on their phone, which they put to work when they were both out. Lydia should have done that if she'd gone somewhere. Then he guessed that she must have been buried under phone calls for him from the many media people who'd have wanted some comment. Lydia had probably gone to the office without activating the machine.

The offices of Julian Quist Associates on Park Avenue were only a couple of blocks away from Garvey's apartment. Quist walked there, the hot afternoon summer sun reminding him that there was another world beside the one of death and destruction he'd been living in for the past hours. He was almost tempted to stop, sit on a doorstep, and drink it in. He didn't.

The glamorous Miss Gloria Chard, receptionist for Quist Associates, looked relieved when she saw her boss walk in from the outer hall.

"We thought you might not be coming in at all, Mr. Quist," she said. "The whole world, it seems, has been trying to get to you. How awful about Miss Hargrove!"

"And the others," Quist said. "A lot of good people senselessly killed, Gloria. Will you ask Lydia if she'll come to my office?"

"I don't think she's come in, Mr. Quist," Gloria said.

Quist stopped in the archway that was at the mouth of

the corridor that led back to his private office. "Not here?" he asked, scowling.

"She hasn't come in, Mr. Quist, but she's probably been in touch with Connie on your private line."

Connie Parmalee was Quist's private secretary, a tall, slim, red-haired girl with an elegant pair of legs that were perfect when mini skirts were in style. Tinted, gold-rimmed granny glasses tended to hide provocative gray-green eyes. Like many girls in her position, Connie was hopelessly in love with her boss. With Lydia, obviously the woman of his choice, with him constantly, in working hours as well as leisure time, Connie was never allowed to forget just how hopeless her feelings for Quist were. The only way she could have a share of him was to be super efficient at her job, indispensable in the work phases of his life.

Connie was waiting for Quist in his office when he got there. That office, with its modern furniture and modern art, was more nearly her home than the apartment where she lived. She looked at Quist and knew that he'd been hit hard. She didn't ask, but produced coffee for him and waited for him to speak. Seated at his desk, he looked up at her with a tired smile.

"Hell to pay," he said.

"I'm so sorry, Julian." She used his first name when they were alone together.

He hesitated. He regretted the necessity of keeping a secret from her. He could have trusted her with it, he knew, but Kreevich had been so insistent—no one but Lydia!

"What we have to do now, Connie, is undo three month's work. Notify people that all programs involving Elissa are off."

"If they can read, or hear the radio, or watch the TV, they don't need to be notified," Connie said. "Wouldn't you be better off to get some rest and tackle this tomorrow?"

"We've got to keep going over everything we've got on

Elissa. There's just a chance there may be some kind of clue that hasn't jumped out at us yet."

"Lydia took a lot of what we had to you and Mark Kreevich—yesterday," Connie said.

"I know. Lydia hasn't come in, Gloria tells me."

"I supposed she was with you," Connie said.

"Not since breakfast. I left her at the apartment. She isn't answering the phone."

"Self-preservation, I imagine," Connie said.

A little red light blinked on Quist's desk. It was the private phone Gloria had mentioned. The office switchboard covered all business calls and interoffice stuff, but Quist had a private phone with an unlisted number that only a very few special people had. Connie picked up the private phone and answered. She frowned as she held it out to Quist.

"Some guy who says he has a message for you from Lydia. Must have gotten the number from her." Connie handed the phone across the desk.

"Hello," Quist said.

"Mr. Julian Quist?"

"Yes."

"There is someone here with a message for you. Will you hold on, please." It was a crisp, New York-sounding voice, but not familiar to Quist.

What followed was totally unexpected, a deep, heavily accented foreign voice. "You will listen without any interruption, Quist, if you care at all about the safety of your Miss Morton."

Quist sat bolt upright in his chair, pointed a finger at Connie, and drew circles with it in the air. She understood and instantly switched on the machine that would record the conversation.

The thickly accented voice went on. "You will withdraw from all phases of the investigation into what happened at the Quatermayne last night. You will withhold any information you may have about Elissa Hargrove that may be helpful to the police. You will—"

"Wait just a minute!" Quist interrupted.

"You wait, Mr. Quist." There was something deadly about the deep voice. "If you follow those instructions to the letter, you may be able to effect an exchange."

"Exchange?"

"Elissa Hargrove for your Miss Morton. You must prepare yourself to arrange for that, Quist. If you are not able to deliver when you get instructions from me, the next time you see your Miss Morton will be in the police morgue."

"How do I know Miss Morton is safe now?" Quist asked.

"You don't. Do as you're told, and she may be. Go to the police with this, and you can begin preparing your lady's obituary."

"I'm just to sit and wait to hear from you?"

"I hope you care enough for the lady to do just that. Goodbye, Quist."

The phone was disconnected, the dial tone buzzing in Quist's ear.

Part
TWO

1

The sound of the dial tone still came from the receiver Quist still held in his hand. He realized that, as he had listened to the threatening voice, he had slowly risen from his chair and was standing behind his desk, rigid, frozen.

Very slowly he put the phone back on its cradle and looked at Connie. She couldn't have heard the conversation, the sound of the voice, perhaps, but not the words. But she had heard Quist ask how he could know that Lydia was safe.

"What's happened, Julian?" she asked.

"God help me, I've got to trust someone, Connie. Play back the conversation."

She rewound the tape and started it playing. Quist turned away, as though he could hear better if he wasn't watching Connie's reaction.

It was all there, not a nightmare. "You will listen without any interruption . . . if you care at all about the safety of your Miss Morton. . . . You will withhold any information you may have about Elissa Hargrove that may be helpful to the police. . . . you may be able to effect an exchange. . . . If you are not able to deliver . . . the next time you see your Miss Morton will be in the police morgue. . . . Go to the police . . . and you can begin preparing your lady's obituary . . ."

"Lydia's been kidnapped!" Connie said.

Quist nodded, still turned away from her.

"I don't understand, Julian. You are to exchange a dead Elissa for a live Lydia?"

Quist turned back to face her. "What you've just heard, Connie, and what I'm about to tell you, you must keep to yourself, or it may cost Lydia her life."

"Of course, Julian."

"Elissa Hargrove isn't dead. She wasn't in the theater when it was bombed. She's alive and well and hidden away in Dan's apartment, guarded by him and the police."

"Julian!"

He explained to her, quickly, how it had all happened. "First only Dan knew, then Lydia and me, then Kreevich. Now we know that somebody else knows. As you said, exchange a dead Elissa for a live Lydia wouldn't make sense."

"But—?"

"This creep on the phone—I'm supposed to figure out a way to get Elissa away from Kreevich and his men and deliver her to him. If I don't—" He turned away again.

"So you go to Kreevich. The whole police force will—"

He spun around. "No!" he almost shouted. "Not till I've had a chance to think it through, Connie. If they know Elissa is alive, they may have some way of knowing whether I'm following their instructions or not."

Connie's mouth thinned out into a straight line. "If you follow the man's instructions, you rescue Lydia from a killer—and deliver Elissa to him!"

"Lydia is all that matters on earth to me, Connie," Quist said. "If I could put a name to the voice on that tape, I'd commit a murder without batting an eyelash!"

She reached out a hand to him and, then, jerked it back, as though she'd been burned. She couldn't risk touching him and possibly revealing what she had to keep hidden—how much she cared for him.

"You've got to think sensibly about this, Julian," she said.

"How do you think sensibly about something that doesn't make any sense?"

"How could they kidnap Lydia?" Connie asked. "They couldn't take her out of the apartment building without attracting attention."

"Between there and here," Quist said. "On the street, a taxi waiting for her to signal. Lydia's not a fool. Stick a gun in her ribs, and she wouldn't resist until she saw a moment where it might succeed."

"There's no reason for this, except to force you into betraying Elissa. They don't ask for money or anything else."

"They want Elissa."

"And you can't sell her out."

Quist's face was a stone mask. "I could sell out the President of the United States, if it was the only way to save Lydia," he said.

"So—how do you get her free of Kreevich and Dan and the cops?"

Quist turned away and walked over to the window that looked down onto Park Avenue and its streams of traffic. After a moment or two he turned back. "Thanks, Connie, for letting me sound off," he said. "When you can't do anything, you talk big."

"But there are things you can do," Connie said.

"Tell me."

"In most situations where there's a threat, you counter it with a threat."

"The trouble is I don't know who he is, where he is, or what he is!"

"So that's what you have to find out."

"My dear Connie—" He let it lie there.

"You haven't been to your apartment," Connie said. "Lydia may have left some message for you there that might help explain—"

"Of course!" Quist started for the door.

"You say Elissa was making some sort of a list for

71

Kreevich—people from the Middle East who might have had it in for the Hargroves. Surely you can get a look at that list without revealing any of this. Somebody on that list is here, in New York, making phone calls—?"

"Could be." Quist turned for the door again.

"And, Julian!" He stopped and she went on. "Remember an actor we used in some of our promotions, Luis Van-Deusen? A language specialist. Dubs in foreign languages on American films? Speaks five or six languages, as I remember."

"What about him?"

"Let him hear this tape. When he hears that accent, he might be able to tell you where it comes from."

"I couldn't trust him to hear the tape."

"Why not? He's a decent man. He'd know Lydia's life might depend on keeping a secret."

Quist walked back into the room and took Connie's shoulders in his hands. She stood straight, hands at her sides, fighting the urge to embrace him, comfort him.

"Bless you," he said and bent down to kiss her cheek. "Try to get VanDeusen here, will you? I'll go to the apartment. Be back as soon as I've checked it out."

A taxi from the office to the Beekman Place apartment was only a few blocks, but quicker than walking. He sat huddled behind the driver, feeling as chilled as though it were winter and not a hot August day. Connie had pulled him back from the brink of something like insanity. She'd made him see that he had to do something practical, something real. Lydia, the cornerstone of his life, was in terrible danger, and only the right action by him could save her. Counterattack or total acquiescence? If he was ordered to get Elissa free of the police and turn her over to the enemy, how could he do it? Would he do it?

What Connie had suggested, without putting it into words, was that he begin by taking the most simple, elementary steps until he had recovered from the shock of learning what had happened to Lydia. Movement forward, of any kind, might help to loosen the knots in his gut, dissipate the fear in his heart that was almost immobilizing.

He looked down at his hands and saw that they were two clenched fists in his lap. He tried moving them, wriggling his fingers. They worked! He opened his mouth to exhale some of the cold air in his lungs, felt a spasm of pain, and realized he'd been clenching his teeth together so hard his jaw muscles were almost locked.

The taxi stopped in front of the Beekman Place apartment building. Quist handed the fare and a tip to the driver. The doorman had the cab door open as Quist prepared to step out.

"Thanks, Dave," Quist said. The gray-haired man in the blue uniform had been working at the front entrance and under the canopy over the sidewalk ever since Quist and Lydia had moved into the apartment here.

"Good to see you, Mr. Quist," the doorman said. "Bad day, huh?"

"Bad," Quist said.

"Everybody in the world has been listening on the radio," Dave said. "Of course, I can't get it out here, but everyone coming and going is talking. Why would anyone blow up that theater and kill so many people?"

"I wish I could tell you, Dave."

"The Hargrove girl was a client of yours, wasn't she? I remember she came here one day—big star, famous beauty. Had us all with our tongues hanging out. Blown up in the explosion, was she?"

"Police are still checking on dead bodies, Dave, but we think so."

"Crazy world," the old man said.

"Tell me, Dave, you see Miss Morton go out this morning? She doesn't answer the phone."

"She went out just after I came on, a few minutes past eight," Dave said.

"Anyone with her?"

"No. She was in a hurry. Asked me to flag her a taxi."

"Did you?"

"Yeah. One was cruising by just then."

"Not one from the cab stand up the street? Not a driver you know?"

"No! Miss Morton was in such a hurry. This guy was just cruising by, and I flagged him."

"No reason you should have checked his license?"

"Gee, no, Mr. Quist. It was a Yellow Cab. But there wasn't any reason I should have—"

"Of course not," Quist said. "If she left a message for me upstairs, it won't matter. I need to find her."

Martin, the man on the elevator, was another longtime employee. Quist spoke before Martin could launch the questions he had when he saw Quist.

"You see Miss Morton go out this morning?" he asked.

"Just after the day shift came on at eight," Martin said.

"She give you any idea where she was going?"

"No, except she seemed to be in a hurry to get there. I— you know—asked her about the bombing. Your name was on the radio, handling promotion for Elissa Hargrove. It doesn't make sense, Mr. Quist—killing so many people."

"Miss Morton didn't give you a hint where she was going?"

"No, sir. Later this guy came with a note from her—to fix the TV."

Quist stopped in his tracks just outside the elevator. "What guy? What TV?"

"Repairman, I guess," Martin said. He fumbled in the pocket of his uniform jacket and produced a folded slip of paper. He handed it to Quist. It was a plain piece of white paper. The writing on it was unmistakably Lydia's.

"Dear Martin: Mr. Bloomfield needs to get into our apartment to fix the television set. I'd appreciate it if you'd get the management key to let him in. Sorry to be so brisk this morning, but I was in a hurry and forgot to tell you Mr. Bloomfield was coming. Thanks. Lydia Morton."

"You let this Bloomfield in?"

"Well, sure. I mean, I showed the note to Mr. Davis, the manager, and he gave me the key."

"Is this repair man still up there?"

"No. He left after about a half hour. Said everything was okay. 'Connection was loose,' he said to me. 'No sweat.'"

"Can you describe him, Martin?"

Martin shrugged. "Nothing special. Short, blond, chunky. Carrying a black bag, which I supposed was his tools. Look, Mr. Quist, I was sure that note was from Miss Morton. Once or twice she'd given me some written messages to deliver to someone she knew was coming, couldn't wait for. The way she shaped the Es."

"Oh, it's her writing, Martin. Greek Es, she called them. She went to school in Europe when she was a kid."

"Then I didn't do wrong?"

"You did what I would have done if I'd been in your place, Martin. Let's go up."

Martin took Quist up to his floor and immediately lowered the elevator down to the lobby level. Quist stood outside his apartment, key in hand, but not moving to unlock the door. The world he was living in wasn't his world anymore. What lay behind that apartment door had been total security, total privacy, revitalization by love and trust—a man's castle! Suddenly, it was as if a large question mark was painted on the door. Lydia wasn't there. He wouldn't be greeted, comforted, encouraged to toss away his problems and relax. In a new world of bombs and mass murder and kidnapping and threats, this sanctuary had been invaded by a stranger who professed to be a television repairman. It didn't make sense. Lydia would never, in the old world, their world, have authorized the building people to admit a workman, unsupervised, into their apartment. And yet, she *had* written the note that the man called Bloomfield had delivered to Martin. That handwriting was as distinctive as a set of fingerprints would have been. She had been under duress, obviously. What kind of pressure had been brought on her? He knew her so well, he was almost certain he could guess how she would have reacted to threats. She was a strong lady, not easily stampeded. There were things in the apartment worth stealing, of course—paintings, antiques, some rare first editions, expensive radio, television, and computer equipment. But it wasn't like Lydia to make it easy for anyone, even if, God forbid, she was roughed up, physically hurt. And Bloomfield, according to Martin, had left as he'd arrived, carrying only his black bag, which Martin guessed had been for tools. He could have carried out a book, maybe some jewelry from Lydia's dressing room. Nothing of great value could have fitted into that bag. If Bloomfield hadn't been there to steal, then what other reason could he have had?

On any other day in his life, Quist would almost certainly not have come up with the answer that suggested itself. He had seen the smoking ruins of the Quatermayne Theater, bomb-destroyed. Bloomfield could have carried some sort of a bomb in his black bag. He had been able to put it in place, unwatched, unsupervised. Would it go off when he put his key in the lock? Would it go off when he switched on the light in the inside foyer? Would it happen when he picked up the telephone or plugged in the coffee machine?

He just stood there, staring at the door. Why would they want to exterminate him? They needed him didn't they? They wanted him to get Elissa free from the police and turn her over to them, didn't they? He couldn't do that dead.

He was, he decided, being an old woman. There had been nothing wrong with the television set when he'd left the apartment that morning. He'd been watching the Quatermayne story just before he'd gone out. It could have happened after that. A tube blows out in a second, a connection shorts. Lydia could have known about a repairman named Bloomfield without ever having mentioned it to him. She could have stopped at the man's place of business, given him the note, sent him on his way.

No way, Quist argued with himself. If Lydia knew the TV had gone sour and intended to send in a repairman to fix it, she'd have mentioned that to Martin on her way out! Second thought, when she was already gone from the building? If she'd known the set was out of order, she might have planned to send in a repairman. But she'd have phoned the apartment manager, or made arrangements before she left the building. It made no sense the way it was meant to look. Lydia was the least scatterbrained person he knew, with the possible exception of Connie Parmalee, his secretary.

No question that Lydia had written the note Bloomfield had handed to Martin. Certainly under pressure, Quist thought. But no amount of pressure could have persuaded her to help let someone into the apartment if she thought it meant some kind of danger for him. No torture, no pain, no threats, could have broken her down, if she thought she was placing him behind the eight ball.

He reached out, inserted the key in the lock, and turned it. Every muscle in his body was tense, but nothing happened except the smooth releasing of the lock and the noiseless opening of the door as Quist pushed it open. He stepped into the vestibule. He reached for the light switch, hesitated, and then turned it on. Nothing but light.

The living room looked perfectly normal when he walked into it. He had thought about things worth stealing as he'd hesitated outside. Glancing around, he saw that all the paintings were in their locations on the wall. No piece of antique furniture was out of place. Some small collector's items were in the glassed-in bookcase where they belonged, along with the several first editions that might have been tempting to a thief.

77

A batch of morning newspapers were on the couch, some scattered on the floor beside it. A china mug on the coffee table suggested that Lydia had been catching up on the reports of the bombing, sipping coffee, when something had interrupted her, obviously taken her out of the apartment. "In a hurry," both Martin and Dave, the doorman, had said. A phone call?

Quist walked over to the desk where the phone was located in this room. There was a message pad in a brass rack beside the phone. The top was blank. According to custom, if Lydia had gone somewhere unexpectedly, she'd have left a message on that pad for Quist. Next to the pad was their personal phone book, numbers written in it that they used frequently, or unlisted numbers of friends and clients. Quist made a quick check under the Bs, looking for a Bloomfield. Nothing. Under TV repairs was the same name of the firm from which they'd bought their television and radio sets, Thomas Farquar & Son. Quist dialed the number.

"Farquar's," a voice answered.

"Tom? This is Julian Quist."

"Oh hello, Mr. Quist. Trouble?"

"Do you have a repairman named Bloomfield?"

"No, I don't. Why do you ask?"

"Some minor problem with the TV," Quist said, "Miss Morton sent in a repairman named Bloomfield. I thought he must be from you."

"No way," Farquar said. "She should have called me, Mr. Quist. You know I'd have sent someone on the double. Did this guy fix it alright?"

"He did what he came here to do," Quist said. "Thanks anyway, Tom."

Quist put down the phone and turned to the television set over by the far wall. He hesitated for a moment and then, almost aggressively, turned on the set. The screen flickered for an instant, and then a perfect picture—of the smoking remains of the Quatermayne. One of the media's top reporters was talking about the irrational savagery of the attack on so many innocent people. If there had been anything wrong with the set, Mr. Bloomfield had obviously fixed it.

It was a day for obscure motivations, Quist thought, as he watched the Quatermayne story unfold on the screen. The commentator was discussing the fact that there was no clear motive for the brutal act of terror. No fanatical group had claimed credit for the bombing, as they so often did after terrorist attacks. Popular choice for the intended victim was Duke Maxwell, although the Hargroves were running not far behind in the public guessing. Followers of the film industry, top figures in the sports world, so-called captains of industry, were all expressing their shock and grief over the mass murders. What was the motive?

Just as obscure to Quist was the motive for forcing Lydia to arrange access to the apartment for Bloomfield, the alleged repairman. He took the note from his pocket that Lydia had written to Martin. Was there a clue there he had missed?

"Dear Martin: Mr. Bloomfield needs to get into our apartment to fix the television set . . . Sorry to have been so brisk this morning, but I was in a hurry and forgot to tell you Mr. Bloomfield was coming. . . ."

That suggested Lydia 'had made arrangements with Bloomfield before she'd left the apartment. Why, then, go to Bloomfield and write the note for him to deliver? The logical thing, if she had forgotten on the way out, was to phone the building management and deliver her instructions in person.

That wasn't, of course, the way it had happened. She had been, somehow, lured out of the apartment, taken prisoner, held against her will. She had been forced to write this note, so that Bloomfield would be admitted. She must have thought of trying to leave some kind of clue in the note, but obviously she'd been forced to write exactly what they told her.

So far nothing had blown up in his face. What else could they have wanted? There had been things worth stealing, but none of them had been stolen. Upstairs, on the second floor of the duplex, was his and Lydia's bedroom, two dressing rooms, two baths, and a small sitting room that was Lydia's private preserve. In Lydia's dressing room there was a jewel case. Expensive jewelry was not her dish, and most of what she kept there was attractive stage jewelry that was simply an adjunct to attractive dressing.

Quist went up the stairs, first to Lydia's room and the jewel case. He had no mental inventory of what it should contain, but there was nothing missing that he would have remembered if it was gone. There was no sign that any clothes had been touched or drawers searched. There was the same result in his own dressing room. Nothing disturbed.

He went downstairs again, to his desk in the living room. He kept no stocks or negotiable bonds here. He had no secret or business papers. Anything of that nature he kept at the bank or in his office safe. The only possible revelation about himself was his personal checkbook. Bloomfield could have discovered what his bank balance was, that was all. And there was no sign that the checkbook had been moved from its place in the desk drawer where he kept it.

Quist stood in the middle of the room, looking around. What in hell had Bloomfield wanted here?

The other thing for which there was no answer was the fact that Lydia had left no kind of message for him. In view of the situation they were in, following the bombing and the discovery that Elissa had escaped it, Lydia's taking off without leaving any kind of message about where she could be reached didn't make sense. Had she been led to believe that she was going somewhere to join him? A message, supposedly from him, could have set her in motion without her leaving any word behind. She would have thought she was headed for him.

His last move was to try the little recording machine on the desk, which he used for dictating business ideas he had when he was out of the office. He set it running. The tape was blank. Lydia hadn't used it.

Where had they taken her? What had they done with her? Could he have missed any kind of clue that was staring him in the face? He sat at the desk for a long time, trying to force something to the surface that wasn't there.

Sitting there was not the answer to anything.

Back at the office, he was greeted by Gloria Chard, the receptionist, with questions about the bombing. Was there anything new?

Only Connie Parmalee, waiting in his office, knew what was really on his mind. He gave her a quick rundown on what he had discovered at the apartment and his total failure to guess why the alleged repairman had gone there.

"There are two people waiting here to see you, Julian," Connie told him. "Luis VanDeusen, the actor is here. Time is running out for him, because he's due to make a recording somewhere. There's time for him to hear the phone call tape through and maybe give you something helpful."

"Bring him in, Connie. You said two people?"

"A woman named Beth Storrs, who says she is—was—Warren Hargrove's executive assistant."

"Tell her I'm back. Ask her to wait. Let's have Luis Van-Deusen first."

Luis VanDeusen was a short little man, balding, with very bright black eyes, suggesting wit and humor. He was a man who'd dreamed of being a great actor and never quite made it. But a marvelous flexible voice and a skill with a number of languages had kept him very busy over the years, particularly on radio in the days gone by and presently in the very special techniques of dubbing in foreign language dialogue for American-made films for foreign distribution. He could imitate an actor's voice so that no one could tell the fake from the original. He had worked for Quist on several overseas promotions, where Spanish, or French, or Italian was needed.

He came into Quist's office, smiling. "I was about to take a powder on you, pal," he said. "I'm supposed to make James Mason sound like a Spanish grandee for an overseas film." Then, sounding exactly like the British actor, he said, "Rather a difficult task, don't you think, old boy?"

"Look, Luis, I want you to listen to about four minutes of a recorded phone conversation. The speaker has some kind of a foreign accent, which I hope you can place for me."

"Four minutes is about what I have," VanDeusen said, glancing at his wristwatch.

Quist gestured to Connie who started the recording machine on the desk. It was all there, the thick accent, the dark threats. Every vestige of humor left VanDeusen's face as he listened. Finally it was over.

"My God, Julian!" the actor said.

"Do I have to tell you that I have to count on you not to pass this along, Luis?"

"Of course not!"

"Where does that creep come from?"

VanDeusen shook his head. "I'm sorry, Julian. When I started to hear what he was saying, I couldn't listen. I'll have to hear it again."

Connie rewound the tape and started it again. VanDeusen leaned forward, intent on what was coming through. "You will withdraw from all phases of the investigation into what happened at the Quatermayne last

82

night. . . . you may be able to effect an exchange. . . . Elissa Hargrove for your Miss Morton. . . . If you are not able to deliver when you get your instructions from me, the next time you see your Miss Morton will be in the police morgue. . . . Go to the police with this, and you can begin preparing your lady's obituary. . . ."

The tape came to the end, and VanDeusen leaned back, wiping at his face with a white linen handkerchief. "It doesn't make sense, Julian. Elissa Hargrove is dead—or isn't she?"

"She's alive and in police custody," Quist said. "Blow that, and you blow the whole thing, possibly Lydia's life! Where does that accent come from?"

VanDeusen drew a deep breath. "In my opinion it's a phony," he said.

"How do you mean?"

"The accent isn't real," VanDeusen said. "Put on for your benefit. If you have the ear for it, you can hear undertones of New York all the way through. Someone from the South Bronx trying to imitate Tony Quinn's Zorba the Greek. Getting it mixed in with a little Spanish, a little Arabic. An amateur with language, unless it was just meant to confuse."

"No way, then, to guess where he comes from?"

"I told you—New York!" VanDeusen said. "Sorry, I can't do better than that, Julian. Is there any other way on earth I can help you?"

"Keep your mouth shut is all, Luis. I'm grateful for your help. You'll be late for your dubbing."

"Mr. James Mason's Spanish grandee will have to wait—if I can be of any use."

"You've already done a lot," Quist said. "You may have saved me from making a tour of the Middle East, trying to hear that voice again on a street corner."

"East of Lexington Avenue above 59th Street is the place

to listen," VanDeusen said. "Knowing what I now know, Julian, you know I'll have to get back to you, to find out if there's any news."

"Connie and I are the only people here who know anything. Don't ask anyone else."

"Good luck," VanDeusen said. He hesitated at the office door. "It just has to work out for Lydia."

"If you believe in prayer, try some," Quist said. As the actor left, Quist lowered his head and covered his face with his hands.

"Shall I put off this Storrs woman?" Connie asked after a moment.

Quist lowered his hands and looked up. "Being associated with the Hargroves, she may have something useful, Connie. Ask her to come in."

Beth Storrs was a woman in her early forties, with dark hair, probably dyed, and blue eyes clouded by pain. Picture of the day, Quist thought—people suffering a deep hurt as a result of senseless destruction. This woman wore a navy-blue suit, smartly tailored, with a white shirtwaist frilled at the collar. Lady executive down to the last detail of her appearance, Quist saw.

"Ms. Storrs?" he said.

"It's Miss, Mr. Quist," she said.

"I'm sorry to have kept you waiting. There's so much whirling around. What can I do for you?"

"I came here in the hope that I might be able to do something for you," Beth Storrs said.

"Oh?"

"There are things Elissa may have told you, as you were getting organized to help her—before the bombing. I thought I might be able to add to them, help substantiate them."

"Shouldn't you be taking anything you have to the police?" Quist asked.

The woman's normally strong, firm mouth twitched at the corners. "I'm in a curious and rather desperate situation, Mr. Quist," she said. "I am—I was"—and her voice broke—"Warren Hargrove's very personal and confidential assistant. Whatever I may know about his business operations, his private life, are sealed away forever—unless—"

"Unless—?" he prompted, when she didn't go on.

"Unless Elissa has told you things, hinted at things. She—she was never as careful about protecting her father's interests as she might have been. She wasn't always as sure of her facts as she might have been. I might be able to save you and the police endless time chasing down blind alleys."

"You want to help us?"

Her lacquered fingernails seemed to bite into the palms of her hands as she leaned toward him. "I loved Warren Hargrove," she said. "Oh, not romantically, but as a great American, a brilliant business man, an example of how power should be used when it comes your way. Warren Hargrove, had it interested him, would have made a great President of the United States."

"So he did work for the CIA?" Quist asked.

Beth Storrs's face seemed to freeze for an instant. "Elissa told you that?"

"Yes. And at the same time she said the CIA would never admit it. Too dangerous for him and for other covert agents working for them."

She pressed the tips of her fingers against her expertly shadowed eyelids. After a moment she looked directly at Quist. "There are things about Elissa that I'm sure she never told you, Mr. Quist."

"What she told me was mostly material that could be used in a promotion campaign for her play," Quist said. "But there were odds and ends scattered around, mostly to help me counter the campaign Pat Walsh was waging against her—and her father. The CIA thing was part of that."

"Walsh is a dangerous man, Mr. Quist. Anything for a sensational story, no matter how libelous, how far from the factual truth."

"And he had a grudge against Elissa? She made a public joke of his romantic approach to her?"

"There was nothing romantic about that approach, Mr. Quist. Walsh is a sexual animal!"

"What are the things you think she may never have told me about herself, Miss Storrs?"

She nodded briskly, as though she had made up her mind to talk. "I go back a long way, Mr. Quist. I was just a secretary in the Hargrove Company when Margaret Hargrove, Elissa's mother, died. That was twenty-two years ago. Elissa was five years old. Margaret Hargrove died in childbirth, trying to provide Warren with the thing he wanted most in the world, a son. Warren adored his wife. I think it was the kind of love that, for some men, can only happen once."

Quist wondered if the dark lady facing him might have tried to make it happen again and failed.

"About that time I moved into a position of confidentiality in Warren's world. His business life, you understand. I think, in that period of shock and grief for Warren, he must have made it clear to his small daughter how much he'd wanted the son that he could now never have."

"Another wife?"

"Not for Warren. Not ever."

"Rather cruel to his daughter, to let her know how he felt."

"He knew that when it was too late."

"Too late?"

"Too late to prevent its having an indelible effect on Elissa. I can see her now, six or seven years old, trying to play boys' games, throwing a baseball or football. She was marvelous with animals. At ten years old she could ride the wildest bucking bronco. Always performing at something physical where Warren could see her."

"Pretty heartless to ignore a child like that."

"Oh, Warren didn't ignore her. Far from it. He loved her dearly, never let a day go by without spending special time with her, never went on one of his business trips abroad without taking her with him. She was for him, I think, an extension of her mother."

"But not a son?"

Beth Storrs nodded. "Elissa missed a step in Warren's thinking. He wanted a son so badly it hurt, but he had a daughter he truly loved. Elissa decided her father wanted a son instead of a daughter. The truth was, he wanted a son in addition to a daughter. For years Elissa tried to *be* a son. She even worked in one of Warren's factories during summer vacation. A son would know all about the technology of Warren's business."

"Hargrove didn't see what she was trying to do?"

"He saw. I gambled my own future by laying it on the line to him. He just laughed. She was sixteen or seventeen at the time. 'I know, Beth,' he said, 'I know. But she may turn out to be one of the most beautiful women in the world, and biology will take over! The woman in her will knock off the fun and games of trying to be a boy.'"

"And he was right?"

"She certainly became a symbol of female sex," Beth Storrs said. "Whether it was biology or sheer accident, it's hard to tell."

"What kind of accident?"

"Hamilton Granger, the Hollywood director-producer, was about to make his *Miss Marvel* movie. The heroine was to be a sort of superwoman. Partly as a promotion, partly as means of finding someone who could do all the athletic tricks required, he staged a series of auditions all around the world. One of them was held in Paris, a summer that we were there on business. We saw the story in the paper, and Warren teased Elissa about it. He pretended to believe she could never outride, outswim, outdive, outfight male stuntmen, the way the French girls who would compete could. Without telling Warren, Elissa went to the audition. I guess Hamilton Granger just took one look at her and knew he'd found what he was looking for. She could not only do all the physical things required of Miss Marvel, she was beautiful, and she could act! She'd been acting all of her life, you see—trying to be someone she wasn't. The result was a multiple-year contract, and she was a star. She had done something that maybe even a son wouldn't have done. She had made it on her own, without Warren's help."

"He was pleased with her?"

"Delighted. Pleased and proud. As you know, Mr. Quist, when that bomb went off last night at the Quatermayne, she was at the top of the ladder. In the whole history of films—Douglas Fairbanks, Mary Pickford, Greta Garbo, Clark Gable—more people have seen Elissa's films than any other star, past or present. Thanks to television reruns, of course. To end the way it did, with Warren there to watch her—oh my God, Mr. Quist!"

Quist found himself stirring restlessly in his chair. Elissa's history was interesting, would have been fascinating to a psychoanalyst, but just now, to him, she was just a bargaining piece in a deadly game that involved Lydia's survival.

"I'm sorry, Miss Storrs, but all this talk about Elissa's childhood and her later problems with her father would be fascinating at any other time," Quist said. "Right now our main concern is trying to identify a mass murderer."

"Ask me what you want to know, and I'll answer if I can," she said.

It was hell not to be able to tell her what *he* knew—that Elissa was alive, that someone connected with the bombing knew and was holding Lydia hostage.

"This talk about the CIA. Was Warren Hargrove working for them or with them?"

She looked away, her eyes lowered. "I can't answer that, Mr. Quist."

"Can't or won't?"

"Can't."

"Because you don't know, or because it was a secret you promised to keep?"

She kept looking down without answering.

"Is it possible you don't really know?"

"In all the years I worked for Warren," she said, after a moment, "all kinds of information came my way. That information came to me, classified by Warren. It was as if he said, 'This you know—and this you don't know.'"

"And you would let his murderer go free rather than tell me what you 'don't know'?"

"Warren trusted me with things that affected his business, his personal safety, perhaps even national security," Beth Storrs said.

"Is that a way of telling me the CIA story was for real?"

"It's a way of telling you that Warren's death doesn't release me from secrecy that was imposed on me."

Quist stood up. "Then there isn't much point in going on with this conversation, is there, Miss Storrs?"

She didn't move from her chair. "You haven't asked me the key question I expected you to ask, Mr. Quist. You haven't asked me whether I think the bombing was aimed primarily at the Hargroves."

"So I ask," Quist said.

"Very frankly, I don't," she said. "Not that the people responsible are weeping any tears over the fact that Elissa and Warren were among the victims."

"Just spell it out, Miss Storrs," Quist said. "I'm running out of time. We're all running out of time. The bomber could be in Timbuktu by now."

"But not the man who paid him. I think the target was

certainly Duke Maxwell," Beth Storrs said. "Indirectly that involved Warren. He was a part of Duke's empire. He was a sports enthusiast. Wherever he could be a part of Duke's world, he took it, invested, helped promote. It wasn't that he expected to get rich by owning a piece of Duke's football team, or putting up money for some of the big fights Duke promoted, or financing the stadium where the football team plays and where many of the big fights were held. It was just that he wanted to be part of a world for which he'd had an enthusiasm since he was a small boy. When Duke decided to go into the theater business and bought the Quatermayne, Warren put some money into it."

"Not sports," Quist said.

"I think he had Elissa in mind," Beth said. "By chance she came up with a play in time to be the attraction for the opening of the new Quatermayne."

"So Duke Maxwell decided to produce the play as a gesture of gratitude toward an old friend?"

"I don't think so, Mr. Quist. *Undertow* is a great play; Elissa was a great star. If anything, it was Warren who did Duke the favor. Elissa and *Undertow* would have been a gold mine for Duke."

"So someone hated Duke enough to prevent that from happening?"

"I don't think so."

"Why, then?"

"Duke lived a very complex life," Beth said. "He dealt with gamblers, gangsters, heaven knows who else. I've heard rumors that a lot of his money came from drugs. Drugs come from other countries, other societies—places where terrorism is an everyday fact of life. Maybe he double-crossed someone. Maybe what happened last night not only wiped him out, but passed along a message to someone else."

"Who?"

"I tell you, I don't know, and this time I *don't* know," Beth said.

"So we're no closer than when you started talking, Miss Storrs. I'm afraid I've run out of listening time."

She stood up, moved toward the door as if she wasn't quite decided to leave. At the door she turned.

"There is a man, Mr. Quist, named Karl Jansen, who might be able to answer some of your questions."

"Who is he? Where do I find him?"

"I don't know, Mr. Quist. But Fred Vail, Duke Maxwell's lawyer, might be able to tell you."

"Damn it, Miss Storrs, I can't waste time on some kind of wild goose chase. What is it you think this Karl Jansen could tell me—if I could find him?"

"I don't know, Mr. Quist." She drew a deep breath. "One night, a couple of weeks ago, Warren and I were having dinner together. Elissa had already gone into rehearsal for *Undertow*. Warren was laughing about Duke Maxwell and all the colorful people he dealt with. I said something about, in the long run, a gambler has to lose. 'The wheel isn't always fixed,' I said. Warren laughed. 'In Duke's case that may not hold,' he said. 'A man with Karl Jansen in back of him isn't likely to lose the big bets.' 'Who is Karl Jansen?' I asked him. Warren just laughed again. 'Jansen is Duke's lucky piece,' he said." Beth gave Quist a steady look. "He didn't choose to elaborate, but he didn't suggest this was something I 'didn't know' or 'hadn't heard.' So, for what it's worth—"

She turned and walked out of the office door.

2
Connie Parmalee came in from her own private office, which adjoined Quist's.

"Get it all?" Quist asked her.

"On tape," Connie said. "I expected you to warn her she was being taped. You always do tell people when you're taping a conversation."

"I don't always have Lydia hanging out on the line to dry," he said, fierce anger barely concealed. "What do you make of her, Connie? Did she come here to help us or to lead us down a dead-end street?"

Connie gave him a tight little smile, but didn't answer for a moment.

"She certainly tried hard to get me off the Hargroves and onto Duke Maxwell," Quist said.

"If something had happened to you," Connie said, frowning, "there are things I would want to keep covered about your personal life, your professional life."

Quist sounded impatient. "Like that I snore?"

"I've never had the opportunity to find that out," Connie said. "Like your will, which was dictated to me, and which I signed as a witness. It's nobody's business what you plan to do with what you leave. If the police were looking for your killer, I wouldn't point a finger at Lydia just because you're leaving her everything you own! There are also intimate secrets about people you've worked for: sexual deviations, drug-taking, strange partnerships, and deals. I wouldn't feel free to talk about those clients and their lives, information that we got in confidence."

"Beth Storrs knows whether Warren Hargrove was involved with the CIA," Quist said. "The fact that she went all around the bush about that indicates to me that he was."

"Or that, if you wanted to know that, you should go straight to the horse's mouth," Connie said.

Quist brought his clenched fist down hard on his desk. "If I'm being watched, they'd know I wasn't following instructions, that I was working on the case. I can't risk that, Connie! Damn! I've got to risk it, don't I? I can't just go home and take a nap, while they do what they want to with Lydia!"

He was hurting so badly, Connie could hardly resist going to him, trying to comfort him.

"Are you asking for advice, Julian?" Her voice was flat, revealing nothing of what she felt.

"What can I lose?"

"You can't go to the one person who could help you, Mark Kreevich," she said. "If the people who have Lydia are watching you, that might appear you were breaking the rules."

"I could call him on the phone."

"How can you be sure about phones? With the money these terrorists have to spend, even police headquarters might not be safe. Dan's phone could easily have been tapped."

"Farfetched, but go on," Quist said.

"Let's assume for a minute that Beth Storrs was playing it on the level with you. Let's assume that Duke Maxwell was the principle target in the bombing. Then it would be safe to guess there is someone named Karl Jansen who might have some answers. Duke's 'lucky piece,' Warren Hargrove called him."

"If he has answers, and he's on the level, he will have gone to the police," Quist said.

"But you won't have the answers if you can't contact Mark Kreevich."

"So?"

"Karl Jansen isn't in the Manhattan phone book," Connie said. "I looked while I was waiting for Beth Storrs to go. But there is someone who might be able to tell you about him, might be eager to help."

"Who?"

"Sandra Cleaves, Duke Maxwell's girl. She's hurting almost as badly as you are, Julian."

"Kreevich has probably seen her already."

"But would he have known to ask her about Karl Jansen? If he didn't ask her, would she have had a reason for mentioning any of Duke's special friends. He would have been asking her about enemies, not 'lucky pieces.'"

"Bless you, Connie, it's worth a try," Quist said. "I'll call her and try to set up a meeting. See if she's listed in the book. If she isn't, we can locate her through Marty's Mansion where she's singing."

"She won't be singing tonight," Connie said, thumbing through the telephone directory. "She's not listed here, Julian."

"I'll go over to Marty's and ask how I can find her," Quist said.

"Let me go, Julian. If you're being watched—"

"The phone. Call them," Quist said.

She didn't move. "You mind if I tell you something quite crazy, Julian?"

"What else is there today?"

"I've been thinking about your Mr. Bloomfield," Connie said. "You say nothing was disturbed in the apartment, nothing out of place?"

"Nothing."

"Did you check the telephone?"

"How do you mean, check it? I used it to call the radio television shop—Farquar's."

"The people who have Lydia have to keep tabs on you, Julian. Where would you make any private or secret telephone calls? From your apartment. It might be worth taking apart the instruments in the apartment to see if you've been had. You go there. I'll check on Sandra Cleaves. Maybe we'll get somewhere."

It was, Quist knew, meaningless, like everything else in the past twenty-four hours, every lock examined after the horse has been stolen. Kreevich and Captain Stewart working themselves to the bone after forty-two people were dead, firemen putting out a fire after buildings were destroyed, and here he was, trying to do something after Lydia was gone. Probably the best thing in the world for him to do would be to go sit somewhere, in public, and wait for orders. But doing something, no matter how trivial, seemed to ease the almost unbearable anxiety for Lydia. His phone was bugged or it wasn't, what difference did it make? If it was bugged, what could he do about it? De-bug it, and make the man with the phony accent unhappy? Go to the police, and instantly put Lydia in greater danger? Well, at least he would know that someone was listening—or wasn't.

Sandra Cleaves, her man blown into small pieces by an act of cowardly terrorism, would probably have nothing to offer but tears and hysterics—or a terrible need for revenge, a need that Quist was feeling now, directed at Lydia's abductors. You point your gun at a hundred shadows and have no idea when to pull the trigger. Sandra Cleaves would be full of stories about Maxwell; in passing, she might know something about one Karl Jansen—whom Beth Storrs had mentioned, in passing. There was a faint chance that might get them somewhere, if they dared to act on any information they got. Hamstrung! And yet Quist knew he'd go crazy just sitting and waiting.

The late afternoon sun was promising a bright evening

sunset. "Red sky at night, sailor's delight." Red was also for blood, scattered over a city block not far away. Red was for terror, and for what might happen to Lydia if he played it recklessly.

The apartment house on Beekman Place had been "home" for a long time, a place of love and certainty, contentment. It was suddenly cold and forbidding to Quist, as he walked across the street to the entrance. Dave, the elderly doorman, greeted him.

"Anything new, Mr. Quist?"

"Nothing," Quist told the elderly man. Nothing! The whole world was new and frightening. Lydia wouldn't be upstairs waiting for him. She might never again be upstairs waiting for him, if he didn't play his cards the way he was ordered to play them.

Martin, the elevator man, stopped him as he crossed the lobby. "I was just going off, Mr. Quist. There's a lady over there been waiting a couple of hours for you to show. I told her I had no way of knowing when you'd come home, but she insisted on waiting."

Quist glanced across the lobby space. Sitting in an armchair by the far wall was a red-haired girl with a pert, Irish-type face. Her legs, encased in pale-blue summer slacks, were crossed, jiggling impatiently. As Quist started toward her, she stood up. Before he reached her, she was holding out her hand to him.

"Mr. Quist? I am Sandra Cleaves."

He should have recognized her. He had seen her perform at Marty's Mansion, but theatrical makeup and costumes created a different image than this simply dressed, rather harrassed-looking girl.

"Coincidence," he said. "Yes, I'm Julian Quist, and at this very moment my secretary is trying to find out how to locate you."

"I'm not in the phone book. Unlisted number. Right now

96

Marty's won't tell your secretary anything. Most of the reporters and gossip columnists in the world have been trying to get to me. I needed to be alone. Marty agreed to help."

"They tell me you've been waiting here a couple of hours."

"They wouldn't be looking for me here," Sandra said. "Safe a place as any."

"The police?"

"Early on," Sandra said, a bitter edge to her voice. "Blind men looking for ghosts in the dark. Can we talk somewhere, Mr. Quist?"

"Of course. My place—upstairs."

Nothing was altered when Quist let them into the apartment. If Mr. Bloomfield had come back, armed with Lydia's keys, there was no sign of it. If Bloomfield had Lydia somewhere, why hadn't he used her keys in the first place? Because Martin and the building management wouldn't have let him upstairs without some kind of authorization. So Lydia had been forced to write the note.

Quist led the way out onto the little terrace that overlooked the East River and gestured to a wicker armchair.

"Drink?" he asked.

"No, thanks."

"I wanted to ask you something, and you came here to ask me something, or, hopefully, tell me something. Who goes first?"

"You were very close to Elissa Hargrove," Sandra said.

She didn't know the truth. Elissa was dead for her. "She was a client," he said.

"But must have had to tell you many intimate things about herself? You see, I know why you were hired to represent her."

"I hope because I'm good at my job," Quist said.

"You were hired to counteract all the gossip Pat Walsh

97

has been spreading about her for the last couple of years," Sandra said. "Miserable jerk!"

"You know him?"

"Doesn't that description fit him?"

"From what I've seen of him, yes," Quist said.

"Of course, I've read his news stories for a long time," Sandra said, "but I never met him until Duke decided to produce this play with Elissa. And then he was everywhere, trying to find out what any of us knew about Elissa's private life. Who were her friends? Who were the men in her life? Almost literally, how many times a day did she go to the bathroom? A monster, that man."

"You didn't come here to tell me about Walsh," Quist said.

"Maybe I came here to be like him," Sandra said, her bitterness almost acute. "I have only one thing left in life of any interest to me, Quist. I want to get my hands on the bastard who killed Duke!" She held out her hands, fingers crooked, scarlet fingernails like claws. "I want to tear out his eyes! I want to hear him scream for mercy!"

"I can understand that," Quist said. He was feeling much the same way, for a different reason, a reason he had to keep to himself.

Sandra relaxed, leaning back in her chair. "It's easier to talk about my anger, my rage, than to give up and weep over what's in my heart. I loved Duke, and I think he loved me."

"If it's any comfort to you," Quist said, "Elissa told me that Duke told her he was a one-woman man, and you were that woman." Not entirely the truth, a one-at-a-time man, Duke had told Elissa.

"Thanks for that, Quist," Sandra said. "What else did she tell you about Duke? That's why I'm here, to ask that."

"Nothing that adds up to anything," Quist said. "That he was a friend of her father's. Her father had invested in some of Duke's ventures—the football team, the rebuilding of the Quatermayne Theater. I supposed it was that friendship that brought Elissa and her play to Duke."

"Nothing else?"

"Like what? I don't know what you're fishing for, Sandra."

Her face was suddenly like a frozen mask. "What happened at the Quatermayne wasn't mischievous kids throwing a brick through a window for the hell of it," she said. "I talked to the bomb squad people. It was elaborate, deliberately planned. It was aimed at Duke, to destroy him and millions of dollars of what he owned."

"It could have been aimed at the Hargroves."

"Never!" she said. "What did they have to lose?"

"Their lives," Quist said quietly.

"All the people who died backstage were Duke's people," Sandra said. "Carefully chosen, trusted people. Duke's people! The only person close to him who didn't die in that massacre was me!"

"Are you afraid that you may still be on someone's hit list?" he asked.

She nodded, without speaking.

"Then you must know something that would make you dangerous to the bomber."

"I don't, Quist. But that doesn't mean that they don't think I do."

"He kept secrets from you?"

"Hundreds, I imagine," she said. "What we had, Duke and I, was just us—what we had together. Fun and games, pleasure, sex. He never talked business to me, or about anything in his other world that wasn't public property."

"Gambling? Drugs?" Quist suggested.

"Duke would bet on anything—a turtle crossing the road," she said. "But not drugs. He had a passion about them and people who used them or dealt in them. He would walk out on a party where he suspected people were using coke. He fired two star players on his football team who were caught using. Drugs, to Duke, were the original sin. He would have turned in his best friend to the cops if he thought that friend was dealing."

"Could that be the motive?"

"I don't think so, Quist. He made no secret about how he felt. No one who knew him would have risked letting him know they had anything to do with drugs."

"They are a way to get rich. Duke Maxwell was rich, and it wasn't oil, or steel, or munitions."

"Like Hargrove?"

Quist nodded.

"Duke was rich because he was lucky. He used to say, 'Because I'm psychic.' He could walk into a gambling casino, put five bucks in a gambling machine and hit the jackpot on the first try. I never knew him to lose an important bet. He even hit the winning number in the state lottery. Three million dollars, they said! The only one out of thousands of ticket buyers who had the right number. He wasn't killed because he was lucky, Quist. Nobody would have gotten anything back from him by killing him."

"So what did you think I could tell you?"

"I don't know. Something that Elissa and Warren Hargrove told you."

"Nothing that adds up," Quist said, "except the one thing I wanted to ask you, the reason I was looking for you."

"So ask."

"Do you know a man named Karl Jansen?"

She frowned, nodding slowly. "A friend of Duke's. I met him a couple of times."

"Who is Jansen? What is he? He was described to me as Duke's 'lucky piece.'"

"He was in Marty's Mansion one night. Duke was there, taking in my show. He loved to watch me do my thing.

Afterward, when I'd joined Duke at his table, Jansen joined us. He and Duke seemed to be old buddies. Very much the gentleman, like Harvard, if you know what I mean. They talked about nothing in particular, politics, I think. At the time I had the feeling Jansen was someone high up, a lawyer, a judge, some kind of government official."

"You asked Duke about him later?"

"He just laughed and said what you said. 'He's my lucky piece. If I ever want a favor from the President of the United States, Karl is the boy who could get it for me.'"

"That's all? No details?"

She shrugged. "I had no reason to be interested. I met this Jansen once again. We were having lunch at Willard's Backyard, and Jansen turned up there. That time he just stopped at our table, said hello, didn't stay to talk."

"You asked Duke about him again?"

"Not really. I just said to Duke, kidding of course, that I'd always wanted to have dinner at the White House. Duke said, if he thought I was serious, he would get Jansen to arrange it."

"That's all?"

"I tell you, Quist, I had no interest in him. I couldn't go anywhere in public with Duke without some stranger coming up and giving him the old buddy-buddy treatment. Jansen was just one of them."

The phone in the living room rang. Quist excused himself and went in to answer it. It was Connie.

"I had no luck on what I was up to," Connie said. "You get done what you went over there to do?"

"Not yet," Quist said. "Believe it or not, when I got here I found Sandra Cleaves waiting for me in the lobby. We've been talking ever since, and I haven't had time to—"

"Damn!" Connie said, and the phone went dead. She'd hung up on him.

He stood there, frowning as he put down the phone. That wasn't like Connie. Then it slowly dawned on him. If his phone was bugged, he'd supplied Bloomfield & Company with something they might want to know.

From the bottom drawer of the desk, Quist took a small screwdriver from a tool kit he kept there. He turned the phone over in his hand and unscrewed the bottom plate. There was the answer to Mr. Bloomfield. The phone had been tapped. Quist hesitated a moment and then screwed the plate back in place without disturbing anything. To disconnect the tap would be to warn them that he knew. Leave it as it was, and the phone might be used to mislead them.

He dialed the office and asked for Connie.

"Sorry for what happened," he said, before she could speak. "Trying to balance the phone and a drink in one hand, and I dropped them both. We got cut off."

"Oh," Connie said, in a distant voice.

"You'd just asked me if I got done what I came over here to do. The answer is, I have. And, of course, you were right."

"Then you—?"

"There seemed no reason to change anything," Quist said. "I'll be back at the office very shortly. Take care, Connie."

Quist went back onto the terrace. He was suddenly concerned about the girl who was waiting for him. She was, she had said, the only person close to Duke Maxwell who hadn't died in the bombing. Had the terrorists been looking for her and not found her? Now they knew where she was.

"My secretary," he told her. "Reporting that she hadn't been able to find you and glad to hear that I had. Tell me, Sandra, have you any idea how I might reach this man Jansen?"

"Not the faintest. I tell you, there were just those two casual meetings, and I wasn't too curious." Her smile was twisted. "I really wasn't interested in dining at the White House."

"Do you have a friend you can trust, where you can hole up for a few days?"

The twisted smile seemed to freeze in place. "I should have, shouldn't I? The truth is I've rather let friends slide in this past year that I've been living with Duke. But I guess I can face reporters now."

"I wasn't thinking about reporters," Quist said. "If someone thinks you may know some special facts about Duke—"

"Oh, brother!" the girl said. "You think—?"

"You think of all the possibilities in a situation like this," Quist said. "Tell me, would Duke have an address or a phone number for this man Jansen—and where would he keep it?"

A little shudder shook the girl's body. "Duke always carried a little address book in the breast pocket of whatever jacket he was wearing. It—it isn't likely you'll find any of it left. From what they've told me—oh God, Quist, the police said the only way they could identify what was left was by a gold identification bracelet on the wrist of a severed hand! I gave Duke that bracelet."

"Dig up a friend, go there quickly, and stay hidden," Quist said.

"May I use your phone?" she asked.

"No! I'm sorry Sandra, but I suspect my phone may be tapped. I may already have let the wrong people know that you're here. Go quickly, before they can get someone set up to tail you." He fished in his pocket. "You got change to make a call from an outside booth?"

"Yes."

"Stay in touch with me, Sandra. But don't call me here, only at my office. If I'm not there, ask for Miss Parmalee, my secretary. She's the only one who'll know what the real score is."

It was after six o'clock when Quist got back to his office. Sandra hadn't stalled, apparently understanding the threat he'd hinted at. At the office Gloria Chard had left for the day. The night watchman was sitting at her desk.

"Connie said you'd be coming back, Mr. Quist," the man said. "I just managed to convince a herd of reporters that you wouldn't be."

"Thanks, Ben."

"Wild day," the watchman said. "You hear about something like this happening in London, or Beirut, or Tel Aviv, and you take it for granted. But when it happens in your own backyard—!"

"Hard to accept," Quist said.

"Cowards! You'd give an arm to come face to face with the bastards," Ben said.

"We will, sooner or later. Connie here?" Quist knew he needn't have asked. Connie would have waited all night for him if necessary.

"In her office or yours," Ben said.

Connie was just walking into his office from hers as he arrived there.

"Ben buzzed me that you were coming," she said. "Julian, I'm sorry I hung up on you, but I didn't know how else to stop you from spilling who knows what."

"Thanks—and I should have my head examined," he said.

He told her about finding Sandra waiting for him in the apartment house lobby. He hadn't wanted to check out the phone in her presence, at least until he knew why she was there. "When you called, I just didn't think—"

"I know. Could she help you with Karl Jansen?"

"Yes and no. Met him a couple of times; he was apparently a good friend of Duke's. But no details, except Duke had joked about his having influence with the president! If Duke had an address or phone number, it was probably blown to pieces along with him—an address book he always carried."

"Jeremy Hoyt," Connie said.

She was, he thought, like a computer. Press a button, and she'd come up with the right answer. Jeremy Hoyt was a good friend of Quist's who worked in the State Department.

"See if you can get him. And, Connie, thanks again," Quist said.

Jerry Hoyt lived and worked in Washington. It took Connie a few minutes to locate him at his home there.

"Julian! I've been hearing about you all day on the tube. Horror story, man," Hoyt said.

"In spades," Quist said. "I need your help, friend."

"Fire away."

"I'm trying to locate a man named Karl Jansen. Can you tell me about him, put me in touch with him?" The silence was so prolonged that Quist spoke. "You there, Jerry?"

"Yeah, I'm here. What do you want with Jansen?"

"He was a friend of Duke Maxwell's. It's possible he can tell us things that would be useful. I've come to believe that Maxwell was the main target of the bombing."

Again a protracted silence before Hoyt spoke. "I don't think I can give you an address or phone number for him, Julian."

"It may sound melodramatic, Jerry, but if I say it's a matter of life and death, I'm not kidding. Is this Jansen a straight man, or is he some kind of undercover what-have-you?"

"Let me just say I'd trust him with my life," Hoyt said. "But I can't tell you how to reach him."

"Well, thanks for nothing," Quist said.

"Julian, wait a minute! It's tricky stuff, but let me tell you what I'll do. I'll contact Jansen, tell him you say it's urgent for you to talk to him, and if he's willing, I'll have him call you. Where?"

"My office," Quist said and gave him the number. "Not my apartment under any conditions, Jerry. My phone there has been tapped."

"It'll be yes or no in the next fifteen minutes," Hoyt said. "I'm sorry to be so cloak-and-dagger."

"As long as you help, I don't care how," Quist said.

He sat in his desk chair, staring at nothing across the room, his hands locked so tightly in his lap his fingers hurt. Help any way he could get it was the name of the game. He had to face it, there was no way on earth he could meet the kidnapper's demand, trade Elissa for Lydia. Elissa meant nothing to him, except that she had been an important client; Lydia was his life, his world. Yet he could not be a party to the decision that one of them should die and the other live.

All he had going for him was time, how much he couldn't guess. The phone would ring, and the man with the strange accent would tell him—a day, an hour? Until that call came, he didn't dare be away from the phone, and yet to wait was to do absolutely nothing for Lydia. A city of what—eight million, ten million people? Not a clue of where to start looking for her. She could be just around the corner, and he could spend a lifetime hunting and never come across a trace of her.

There was a knock on the office door, and before Connie could get to it, Ben, the night watchman, opened it and looked in.

"Sorry to barge in on you, Mr. Quist."

"It's all right, Ben. What is it?"

"There's a character out in the reception room who says he has to see you, won't go away till he does. I told him you weren't here, but he says he knows better. He says it's important for him to see you and equally important for you to see him."

"Does he have a name?"

"It's Pat Walsh, the newspaper reporter. I know you don't want to get involved with the press, but this guy is stubborn. If you tell me to get rid of him, it'll have to be a little physical."

If Walsh chose to help, he might be able to, Quist thought. He had spent two years on the complex world of the Hargroves. He might have a lead if he chose to give it. If he came in here, the phone might ring, a call from Jansen or from the kidnapper.

Connie, as usual, read his mind. "If a call comes, you can take it in my office," she said. "I'll set up the phone so the call will be recorded. I'll entertain Mr. Walsh if that happens."

Quist turned back to Ben. "Show him in. But stay close by, Ben."

Quist stood up and walked away from his desk, flexing his tense fingers. "I can't handle this alone, Connie," he said. "I've got to have help from somewhere."

"Dan," she said. "You can tell him what's cooking, trust him."

"While you're setting up the phone, Connie, call him. Tell him I need him."

She hurried out of the office, leaving him alone. A moment later the office door opened, and Ben ushered in Pat Walsh.

"You don't make anything easy, Quist," Walsh said.

"Is there some reason I should?" Quist asked.

"A man who has blown up forty-two people and a theater isn't likely to be bothered by his conscience if he has a reason to strike again," Walsh said. "You and I might be able to put your two and my two together and come out with a four."

"Well, I'll start first," Quist said. "You told me that people all over the Middle East know that Hargrove has been double-crossing his customers out there. Name me one who will be willing to talk about all he knows."

"I'll start first," Walsh said. "Why are the police guarding Dan Garvey's apartment? Why is Kreevich spending time there? Why is a cop patrolling the corridor outside this office? Obviously, Kreevich thinks you and your partner are in danger."

The last was something Quist couldn't explain; the first was something he wouldn't. "How do you know all this?" he asked.

"I'm covering a terrorist massacre," Walsh said. "As a responsible reporter, I want to get to the main man, Lieutenant Kreevich. He, in turn, is trying to duck the press. Well, I wasn't born yesterday. I tried to locate a place where he might light. It turned out to be Dan Garvey's apartment. Cop in the lobby, no way to get to him. Why there? Logically, he should be at police headquarters or at the Quatermayne or at the Hotel Benson, where the cops have set up an on-the-scene office. Instead of that, he spends a couple of hours at Garvey's and then takes off, surrounded by an army of cops. He didn't seem happy when he saw me waiting for him. I figured you'd have to know what it's all about. He doesn't need bodyguards in order to protect you and Garvey unless you know something that places you in danger."

"Does it occur to you that Kreevich is trying to protect himself from people like you—reporters, cameramen?"

"That doesn't explain why he'd spend two hours with Garvey. Garvey's whole life story wouldn't take that long to tell. And that doesn't explain why he'd leave cops to guard Garvey after he'd found out everything he could from him."

Of course it didn't. The cops were there to guard Elissa. Thank goodness, Walsh hadn't come up with anything like the truth.

"I don't have an answer for you," Quist said. "I've been here, trying to put together a dossier on Elissa for the police. Dan, of course, knows a lot about her. Kreevich is digging for everything he can find."

"Bull!" Walsh said. "Garvey may know gossip about Elissa. Everyone in the world does. But you and Miss Morton are the people with facts on her, carefully collected for your purposes. Why isn't Kreevich talking to you?"

An answer that might satisfy Walsh came to Quist. "He has talked to me and Lydia both," he said. It almost hurt him to mention Lydia's name. "But I can make a guess for you. One of the things the police were uncertain about earlier in the day was the question of who was the primary target of the bombing."

"The Hargroves of course."

"One guess. The other is Duke Maxwell. Dan knew Duke well, played on his football team for seven years, has worked with him on sports promotions for this office. Kreevich could have been trying to find out what he could about Duke."

Walsh was frowning, his bright eyes narrowed to slits. "And left cops to guard him after he got the Duke Maxwell story from him?"

"If Dan came up with a lead that could uncover someone, he could be in danger," Quist said.

"I don't think you're leveling with me, Quist! What the hell is going on there at Garvey's place? You don't believe what you just said. Garvey's your best friend. If you thought he was in danger, you'd be over there instead of sitting here, working on Elissa's obituary for Kreevich."

"I've told you what I know," Quist said. "That's my 'two.' Let me have yours, and we'll see if it comes out four. You're so hipped on the Hargroves, you're not willing to look at any other possibilities. You call yourself a 'responsible reporter.' You're really only interested in capping off a personal feud."

Connie was suddenly in the doorway to her office. "I'm sorry to interrupt, Mr. Quist, but the call you were expecting has come through. I can get Mr. Walsh some coffee while you take it in here."

"Don't bother," Walsh said. He called after Quist who was leaving. "You want to keep playing games with me, buster, it's your funeral!"

Quist closed the door between the two offices and picked up the phone on Connie's desk.

"Julian Quist here," he said.

"I understand you wanted me to call you, Mr. Quist." A pleasant, well-modulated, cultivated voice. "My name is Karl Jansen. At least that is a name I use. You might call it a pen name."

"Then who are you, and what are you, Mr. Jansen?"

"I'm not calling you to be interviewed, Mr. Quist," Jansen said. "Jeremy Hoyt persuaded me that you had big troubles and that I might be helpful."

"You've been listening to accounts of a disaster we've had here in New York?"

"I've been doing more than that, Mr. Quist. I've been involved—in a way."

"Involved?"

"Perhaps we will save time if I tell you that I know what one of your problems is," Jansen said. "I know what the situation is at Dan Garvey's apartment. I don't trust your phone or mine, Mr. Quist, so I won't put it into words."

"How do you know?"

"A friend of yours, Lieutenant Kreevich," Jansen said. "He, too, wanted help."

"Mark has been in touch with you?"

"Yes."

"And did you help him?"

"I hope so. You'll have to ask him. Now, what is it I can do for you, Mr. Quist?"

What indeed? Quist found he was having trouble breathing normally. "In a way, Jansen, I am working for Kreevich."

"He mentioned you. Which is why I was willing to call."

"What Mark doesn't know at the moment is that I have received threats."

"Against yourself?" Jansen asked.

"Against a friend of mine."

"Garvey?"

"Let me put it this way, Mr. Jansen. You don't trust the phones. Neither do I. I can only tell you that demands have been made on me that, if I don't meet, a person very dear to me may die."

"That's trouble. You want help in meeting those demands?"

"Yes—no! They can't be met in good conscience. My only hope, Mr. Jansen, is to identify the person who's threatening me before he can carry out his threats. My reason for contacting you is that I'm told you were a close friend of Duke Maxwell's."

"That's not a secret, Mr. Quist."

"Duke, I'm told, called you his 'lucky piece.'"

The faint sound of a chuckle came over the wire. "You knew that Duke won a multimillion-dollar lottery?"

"Yes."

"Four numbers," Jansen said. "Duke chose the last four digits in a telephone number he had for me. Jackpot! That's how I became his lucky piece."

"Is it possible he was the target for the bombing at the Quatermayne?" Quist asked.

Jansen's voice turned from polite to grim. "I would say it was a certainty."

"Why?"

"Let me put it to you this way, Mr. Quist. Duke Maxwell's life-style made him a marvelous front for a far more serious kind of business. Kreevich knows now, the people responsible for the bombing knew, and now you know, that he was working for the government."

"The CIA?"

"Let's just say 'the government,' Mr. Quist."

"Elissa Hargrove told me her father was working for the CIA," Quist said.

"He was, and he wasn't," Jansen said. "We suspected that Hargrove was selling high technology and sophisticated weapons to people in the Middle East we think of as, at the least, unfriendly. We put Duke Maxwell on to him. Hargrove was a sports fan. It was easy for Duke to make friends with him. Duke let Hargrove invest in some of his enterprises. After a while Duke became convinced that Hargrove was not involved in what we'd suspected. In the end Hargrove helped Duke with what he was trying to ferret out in the Middle East."

"You say you've talked to Mark Kreevich and that you know what's going on at Garvey's apartment."

"I have, and I do," Jansen said.

"Then Mark told you that we've been told Hargrove was threatened by the people he'd been dealing with in the Middle East."

"That, at least, is what Hargrove told his daughter," Jansen said.

"That's what I was trying to say—without saying it."

"Let me try to say something—without saying it," Jansen said. "Duke and Hargrove, through his Mideast contacts were hot on the trail of something. Top-level secrecy. What Hargrove told his daughter was, I think, an attempt to explain certain tensions without telling her the real truth."

"You think he wasn't threatened, then?"

"I'm guessing, Mr. Quist. He may have been threatened, but not for the reason he gave his daughter. And the man who threatened Hargrove may have done so knowing that he'd go to Maxwell with it. Maxwell would gather all the people he could trust, or had used, to guard him. That's what they wanted. Maxwell, surrounded by everyone who might know anything all blown to hell with one flip of a switch."

"There's a man in the next office right now who's convinced Hargrove was the primary target—Pat Walsh."

Jansen's laugh was mirthless. "Why do you suppose Hargrove let Walsh slander him and his daughter for two years without bringing some kind of an action against him? Because Walsh succeeded in getting everyone to look in the wrong direction, with his malicious attacks on Elissa and his hints about Hargrove's sinister dealings with the enemy. As long as Walsh didn't smell out the real game, let him have his head."

"You think Hargrove went to the theater last night because he believed Duke was in danger?" Quist asked.

"Could be," Jansen said. "They probably expected a man with a gun, not the end of the world!"

"So we come back to my problem," Quist said. "A person I care for is a prisoner somewhere. I am instructed to exchange someone else for that person—or else."

"Someone at Garvey's apartment?" Jansen's voice had gone rock hard.

"If I could do that, Mr. Jansen, I wouldn't—couldn't. My only hope is for someone to point me in the right direction. Point me in time, Mr. Jansen. That's why Jeremy Hoyt sent me to you." There was a dead silence. "Are you there, Jansen?"

"Yes, I'm here. If I could name a name or a place, I'd give it to you, Mr. Quist. I have given Kreevich everything I have, my personal suspicions, my guesses. Have you told him yet about your problem?"

"No, Mr. Jansen. I've been sitting here sweating, not knowing who I dared go to for help. I was warned against going to the police. I don't dare leave the phone here, for fear I'll miss the next set of instructions from the man who has my friend."

Again a silence, and then Jansen came back. "I have a hunch, Mr. Quist, that you will be given some time. Arranging for an exchange, as you put it, is not a five-minute job. I suggest you do what you would do if you were going to try to make that exchange. Go to Garvey's apartment. Find Kreevich, tell him what the situation is. Get him to tell you what I suspect."

"I'm probably watched, my home phone is tapped, someone Walsh took for a policeman is watching this office. I make the wrong move, and my friend—"

"Your friend is not going to make it, Quist, now or later unless you run risks. One thing I can tell you. Don't waste your time looking overseas to the Middle East for the man you want. My guess is that he is just around the corner somewhere."

"The man who called me about the 'exchange' spoke in what could have been an Arab accent."

"People who tell Jewish jokes, or Polish jokes, or Irish jokes are not necessarily any one of those nationalities—"

New York, Luis VanDeusen had said, unmistakably New York. Jansen was supporting that theory.

"I'm going to give you a number, Quist," Jansen said. "It's a number here in Washington. You won't get me if you use it, but the person who answers can be trusted. You got a pen, paper?"

"Right in front of me on the desk."

Jansen dictated a phone number to him. "If your situation gets down to a question of manpower, Quist, I may be able to help you faster and more efficiently than Kreevich and the Manhattan police force can."

"I'm grateful," Quist said.

"One last thing, Quist. I have learned in my business, which is something that's become a dirty word—covert activities—to always be sure of one thing. The people you confront in a dangerous game are almost certainly not what they pretend to be. The Texas oil man is probably a drug peddler for a heroin factory in Naples; the Midwestern college professor is probably a negotiator between the Irish rebels and the Libyan terrorists who supply them with arms. The millionaire sports promotor like Duke Maxwell turns out to be a freewheeling CIA agent. People are almost always not what they advertise themselves to be."

"My Arab terrorist who threatens my friend is probably the godfather of a criminal gang?"

"Something like that, Mr. Quist. But I suspect it's someone who knows you, knows Garvey, knows Elissa Hargrove, and knows your lady."

"My lady?"

"That's who's in trouble, isn't it, Mr. Quist? Stay in touch if you don't come up with answers for yourself."

End of the line. The phone went dead.

3

Quist sat at Connie's desk, staring at the dead phone. Who was Karl Jansen? He knew things that no one was supposed to know. First, he knew that Elissa was alive. Had Kreevich told him, or did he have other sources? Had he guessed about Lydia, or had he known all along, while Quist spilled his guts? Had Jeremy Hoyt, a man he trusted, whom he thought of as friend, delivered him to his enemy?

The office door opened, and Connie looked in. "I checked the extension and realized your conversation was over. Any luck?"

Quist brought his fists down hard on the desk. "Everybody knows everything—except me!" he almost shouted. "That character knows about Lydia. Maybe just a guess. He knows about Elissa. No guess. He indicated that Kreevich told him. I can't handle this alone, Connie. I need help. This Jansen character says I should go to Kreevich. If I do, the man who has Lydia will probably know and punish me by—by harming her."

"Dan Garvey is your closest friend," Connie said. "Surely you can trust him. He can come here. It's his place of business. No one will know for certain that you sent for him. He could go back to Lieutenant Kreevich and let him know what's going on."

"Walsh?"

"He took off as soon as you left here to pick up the call from Jansen."

"He mentioned a cop who was outside in the hall."

"There was, and there wasn't," Connie said. "I sent Ben outside to check. The building is swarming with cops, but they're not concerned with you."

"How do you know?"

"You're not trusting the people you ought to trust, Julian. Kreevich wouldn't have cops guarding you without telling you. It seems the wholesale jewelers who have offices down the hall—Greenberg & Sons—were robbed. The man Walsh saw, and being a reporter he might have recognized him as a cop, was part of the robbery detail handling the Greenberg case. Walsh assumed he was here watching you, which, of course, he wasn't."

Quist stood up. "See if you can get Dan on the phone. If a cop answers, and Dan isn't there, tell him that I have vital information for Mark."

"Will do." Connie started back into Quist's office.

"Connie!"

She turned back.

"There are people you take for granted. I don't know where I'd be at this moment without you, Connie. I want you to know that."

"Thanks, Julian. Thanks very much."

She went to the phone on Quist's desk and dialed a number. "Dan? Hold on. Julian wants you." She held out the phone to Quist.

"Dan?" Quist asked.

"Hi," Dan said.

"Dan, I need you. Can you come over to the office?"

"I think not, Julian." Dan sounded distant, a little hostile.

"You think not?"

"I'm taking a leave of absence until this mess is cleared up here, Julian. I trusted you, and I shouldn't have. I'm staying here until Kreevich can assure me that Elissa is safe."

"Dan, I've been threatened. Lydia has been threatened. I can't come to you without taking the risk that those threats will be carried out."

"You're a big boy, Julian. You can take care of yourself."

"The threats involve danger to Elissa also," Quist said. "If you don't give a damn what happens to me or Lydia, concern yourself for Elissa."

"What are you talking about?"

"Come over here and find out," Quist said. "The police will guard Elissa." Quist hung up the phone. "End of a beautiful friendship!"

"Don't bet on it," Connie said. "He trusted you with a secret, and he thought you betrayed him. His feelings were hurt. It'll take him ten or twelve minutes to get here."

"Let us pray," Quist said. "Set up the tape of the kidnapper's phone call to me."

Connie was off by about two minutes. It was fourteen minutes later that they heard Garvey's voice calling out something to Ben as he came down the hall to Quist's office.

"If you've suckered me again, Julian—" Garvey said, as he stormed into Quist's office.

"Just sit down and listen," Quist said. He gestured to Connie to start the tape rolling.

It was there again, that heavily accented voice, its demands, its threats. Quist tried to hear the New York overtones that Luis VanDeusen claimed to have heard. He didn't have the ear for it, the expertise. The tape came to an end. Garvey sat where he was, looking frozen. Then he muttered some obscenities under his breath. Then he got up and crossed the room to where Quist stood behind his desk.

"I'm sorry," he said. "I've behaved like a damn fool."

"You put Elissa's safety in my hands, and you think I let

you down," Quist said. "Now I have put Lydia in your hands."

Garvey reached out and put his hand on Quist's shoulder. "Just forget everything, Julian. Tell me what you want me to do, and it's done."

"Thanks, pal."

"I've been behaving like a kid with hurt feelings," Garvey said.

"So let me bring you up to date." He gave Garvey the whole story, first his visit from Beth Storrs, then the tape he had just heard, then the trip to his apartment and finding Sandra Cleaves there and the news that a fake television repairman had been there with a note from Lydia. Then the discovery that his phone had been tapped.

"The note from Lydia, you saw it?"

"She wrote it. With a gun pointed at her head, of course."

Quist went on with his calling on Luis VanDeusen and what the actor had said about the voice. Finally his calling on Jeremy Hoyt and his conversation with Karl Jansen, the mystery man in Washington.

"Mass confusion," Quist said. "If you believe any of it, you have to think the bombing was aimed at Duke Maxwell and possibly Hargrove. The others who died are just incidental."

"Maybe not," Garvey said. "Maybe someone else who knew the score about Maxwell and Hargrove."

"So where do we go from here?" Quist asked.

Garvey shook his head. "It takes a while to absorb it all," he said. "One thing is certain. If your man Jansen is for real, then Kreevich knows more than he's let on to me or Elissa."

"Where is Mark?"

"I don't know. He stayed with Elissa for a couple of hours, getting a list of names from her of people, groups in the Middle East who might have it in for her father. People who might have warned him, threatened him. Then Mark took off, I supposed to go back to the Quatermayne, the Hotel Benson, police headquarters. He didn't say, but he left cops guarding my apartment. I was free to go where I wanted, do what I wanted, but Elissa was to stay put. She—she needed someone, and so I stayed there."

"She's still convinced the bomb was aimed at her father and herself?"

Garvey nodded. "And so was I, until now."

"The killing could have been aimed at them as well as Maxwell," Quist said. "Elissa hasn't mentioned any kind of under-the-table relationship between her father and Duke?"

"No, but, if it was that kind of hush-hush deal, her father might not have told her. It would be the kind of thing that would be dangerous for her to know if someone put heat on her. But damn it, Julian, we're not talking about the main ball game. Lydia! That Arab bastard on the tape—"

"If he is Arab. Luis VanDeusen thinks not."

"VanDeusen couldn't be in on it, trying to mislead you?"

"No one had any reason in the world to guess I would call him," Quist said. "It was Connie's idea. We'd used him, you know, an expert on foreign languages and accents."

The light on the phone blinked. Quist felt himself go tense. A call from Lydia's captors with new instructions? Connie picked up the phone, the look on her face indicating she shared Quist's anxiety.

"Julian Quist Associates." And then she almost smiled as she held out the phone to Quist. "Lieutenant Kreevich," she said.

"Mark!"

"Are you alone, Julian?"

"Just Connie and Dan."

"I understand you've been talking to a friend of mine in Washington, Karl Jansen."

"I'm glad to hear he's a friend. I had some doubts."

"Is what he thinks about Lydia true?"

"He thinks or knows?"

"He guesses, from what you said—and the way you said it."

"Yes, it's true, Mark."

"Stay put," Kreevich said. "I'll be there in a quarter of an hour."

Kreevich listened to the kidnap tape when he arrived. He was a man who had been on the go for more than twenty-four hours, and he looked on the brink of exhaustion, the lines on his unshaven face deepened, his eyes almost glazed.

"Why haven't you tried to get to me? You got this call hours ago."

"It's right there, Mark. I was warned not to go to the police. Lydia is—Lydia is everything to me."

"I know. And as much to me, in a different way," Kreevich said. "Arab-sounding voice." He gestured toward the tape machine.

Quist told him about calling in Luis VanDeusen and the actor's analysis of the call. "And Jansen tells me that nobody, in the world of terrorism, is what he appears to be. Are you a cop, or are you really a secret agent, Mark?"

"Who answered the phone when this call came in?" Kreevich asked. "If it came from overseas, you'd have been told the overseas operator was trying to reach Julian."

"I answered," Connie said. "There was no such announcement. An unaccented voice asked for Julian, and when Julian came on—" She nodded at the tape machine.

"So it could have come from a phone booth downstairs," Kreevich said. "If your friend VanDeusen is correct, it could have been just one man, first without an accent, then playing a phony Arab."

It was the same story, over and over, advancing them not one step closer to Lydia. There was Beth Storrs and her suspicions. There was Sandra Cleaves and her encounters with Jansen. There was Lydia's note and the phony TV repairman who had tapped his apartment phone. And there was Karl Jansen.

Kreevich seemed to pull himself out of a deep hole, something almost like an exhausted sleep. "All that talk of Elissa's about the CIA and her father's deals with the Arab terrorists took me to the only solid source I had," he said. "Karl Jansen. He doesn't have an official title that I know of, but he works at different times for the State Department, the CIA, Justice. He is what I guess you would call an expert on terrorism. He knew of the relationship between Duke Maxwell and Warren Hargrove. His judgement is that the bombing was meant for Maxwell, with Hargrove, hopefully, included."

"What Elissa told us about a warning to her father? He must get up-to-date weapons to his customers or else."

"You have to think Hargrove told his daughter that to cover the real truth," Kreevich said.

"Which was?"

"That Maxwell, his friend, was in danger, and that he would go to the Quatermayne to warn him."

"And stayed there to get killed himself?" Quist asked.

Kreevich shrugged. "Or, since he was there, to watch his daughter act and, incidently, to protect her—just in case."

"A smart operator like Hargrove just making a target of himself?" Quist asked. "Sitting, prominently, in the front row? Walsh saw him sitting there, was waiting to see who might contact him."

"If Walsh is telling the truth," Garvey said.

"Which he wouldn't do if it would get in the way of a story," Quist said.

"He was there, at the back of the house when the bombs went off," Garvey said. "He was seen by Fred Vail, Maxwell's lawyer, by others."

"Let's follow Jansen's advice and turn everybody inside

out," Quist said. "Starting with Fred Vail. He isn't Maxwell's trusted man. He was paid by the terrorists to get Duke murdered. Pat Walsh has been faking his animosity to the Hargroves to cover an involvement with them. Elissa has lied to us to cover her father's involvement with Maxwell. Guardino, the electrician who was getting coffee, was actually a paid hand of the terrorists."

Kreevich's cold glance was directed at Dan Garvey. "I'm going to tell you something that Jansen reported to me, something you're going to find hard to believe," he said. "Jansen's sources in Libya tell him that, when the Hargroves were in the Middle East, with Walsh tailing them to prove out his story about Hargrove's treachery—" Kreevich stopped there.

"So what about it?" Quist asked.

Kreevich drew a deep breath. "Jansen's sources tell him that Elissa and Pat Walsh were lovers."

"Oh, come off it, Mark!" Garvey said.

"I'm telling you what I was told," Kreevich said.

"For two years Walsh has been trying to tear down both Elissa and her old man!" Garvey said. "You only have to go to the newspaper files to verify that. Hints, veiled accusations, the works!"

"A cover, according to Jansen's sources," Kreevich said.

"A cover itself, to turn Jansen away from the real truth," Garvey said. "He should follow his own advice and take a second look at his 'sources.'"

"Perhaps," Kreevich said. "But can we afford to pass it by as malicious gossip? It needs checking out, don't you think? Jansen swears by his informant."

Quist found himself gripping the arms of his desk chair. "That would suggest that Elissa escaped the bombing by faking her laryngitis, that Walsh knew where he would be safe in the theater. Have you checked Elissa's doctor, Mark?"

"Elissa didn't have a personal physician here in New

York. She says she called the stage manager—killed in the blast, by the way—to ask him to recommend someone. The stage manager said he would send someone to her place to check her out. A doctor, according to Elissa, came to see her."

"His name?"

"She doesn't remember. A foreign sounding name, she says—which isn't unusual in New York. The great melting pot? This doctor said the stage manager had sent him. Of course, the stage manager can't verify that. He's gone. The doctor, according to Elissa, treated her with medication he had with him. 'Laryngitis. This will work or it won't,' he told her."

"No prescription that can be checked?" Quist asked.

"No—according to Elissa. If the medication didn't work, she should have a thorough checkup today, somewhere. It didn't work. It didn't work, so she left the theater and got lucky."

"It all sounds perfectly reasonable. She was in a panic about trying to go on stage with no voice. She didn't try to remember a German, or Czech, or Spanish name—or Polish, or Jewish. The stage manager would tell her how to get the doctor back, if she needed him when she got to the theater."

"In view of what happened, isn't it queer the doctor hasn't come forward?" Quist asked. "Or has he?"

Kreevich shook his head. "I've asked Fred Vail if Maxwell had a personal doctor, or there was someone engaged to cover for the theater people. Maxwell's doctor is a well-known Park Avenue boy with the hard to remember name of Brown. There was no company doctor. Whoever the stage manager recommended was his own selection."

"Someone must know who his doctor is," Quist said.

"His family live in California," Kreevich said. "They have no idea who he might have recommended here in New York."

"Are you suggesting she didn't have laryngitis?" Garvey asked. "You heard her talk, try to talk."

"I'm following Jansen's advice," Kreevich said. "I'm assuming nothing is the way it's meant to look. Elissa is an actress. A stage whisper would be duck soup for her, wouldn't it?"

"And she knowingly let her own father be killed?" Garvey asked. "Should we waste time with this kind of nonsense, Mark?"

"What about the list of people Elissa was going to give you, Mark?" Quist asked.

"Middle Eastern terrorists, all of them," Kreevich said. "All authentic, all just the kind of people her father might have been playing games with, if he was playing games. Jansen says he wasn't. And not one of them would admit anything to Western intelligence."

"And you're going to follow this absurd trail, while the real villains go free, maybe preparing to strike again somewhere?" Garvey asked.

"In my business, Dan, you follow all the trails that show themselves," the detective said.

"You expect me to go back to my apartment and not tell Elissa what kind of crap you're playing with?" Garvey asked.

"Tell her, by all means," Kreevich said. "It will be interesting to know what her reaction is."

"I can tell you in advance. She will laugh herself sick."

"If she's recovered enough voice for that," Kreevich said.

"May I remind you two that we're not getting any closer to Lydia?" Quist said, anger in his voice.

As if on cue, the red light on the telephone blinked. Quist gestered to Connie who picked up the extension.

"Julian Quist Associates," she said. She didn't have to tell Quist who it was. She pointed toward her mouth. "Just a minute, please."

Quist gestured toward Kreevich, watched Connie hand

the phone to the detective, and then picked up his own phone. There it was, the heavily accented voice.

"I'm not pleased with the way you're handling things, Mr. Quist," the voice said. "I know that Lieutenant Kreevich is there with you. I'm sure you've told him what your dilemma is."

"You asked me to arrange for an exchange," Quist said.

"And instead you have spoiled your chances."

"Do you expect me to answer that under the circumstances?"

"You mean with the lieutenant listening on an extension?"

"If you believe that, tell him what you expect me to do."

The man on the other end indulged in a short little laugh. "Good evening, Lieutenant," he said. "I'm sure you must be anxious for the safety of your friend's lady."

"More anxious to catch up with you, Buster," Kreevich said.

"That will cost you," the man said. "I tell you how it is, Lieutenant. You will remove the guards from Garvey's apartment in the next hour. You will keep Garvey and Quist from going there. You will do those things, or I will send evidence to Quist that his lady has no more interest in the future."

"How do we know it isn't already too late for Lydia?" Quist asked.

"You don't. But now you know just how far my patience will stretch. Good evening, gentlemen." And the phone went dead.

No one spoke for a moment. Quist was staring at Kreevich, waiting for some comment from the detective. Finally Kreevich spoke.

"One of the most frustrating things the police have to face is the telephone terrorist," he said. "The breather, the man dishing out sexual obscenities to a local housewife, the kidnapper, the voice claiming responsibility for some local violence. There's no time to check on where the call is coming from. You just listen, and eat whatever it is."

"So how is your digestion?" Garvey asked, still bitter.

"Cast iron," Kreevich said. "I've been listening to those kinds of threats for the last twenty years."

"How often are the threats carried out?" Quist asked, in a faraway voice.

"More often than I like to tell you, Julian."

"Please, God—" Quist said and looked away.

"You can't leave Elissa unprotected," Garvey said. "And, incidentally, you can't stop me from going back to my own apartment."

"Oh, I can stop you, Dan," Kreevich said. "I can arrest you, charge you with obstructing justice, and hold you for a great deal longer than an hour before you can get yourself a lawyer, bring charges against me for false arrest."

"You'd do that?" Garvey asked, his anger at the explosion point.

"I don't think I'll have to," Kreevich said. "We haven't got time for anything but to decide, mutually, what we can do, what we will do to save Lydia from what she's facing."

"While the families and friends of forty-two dead people are clamoring for something else, probably going to the mayor, the governor, the president, asking for action," Garvey said.

"So take charge," Kreevich said. "Give me my orders!"

The two men faced each other for an instant, and it was Garvey who broke away. "I'm sorry, Mark," he said. "I love Lydia like a sister. I'm just as concerned as Julian and you are for her safety. But I've been with Elissa for almost a whole day, listening to her story, seeing the staggering blow her father's death is to her, trying to comfort and reassure her. It just doesn't seem possible that you can agree to trade one human life for another—choose to save the one you like best!"

"How can it be," Kreevich asked, "that we can have

known each other so long as we have and you'd think I'd base any decision I make on 'who I like best'?"

"I would. I'd have to," Quist said, sounding very far away.

Kreevich took a cigarette pack from his pocket, discovered it was empty, crumpled it, and tossed it toward a wastebasket. Connie crossed to a wall cabinet, produced a fresh pack of cigarettes, and handed it to the lieutenant. Kreevich nodded his thanks, opened the new pack, took out a cigarette, and snapped his lighter into flame. Quist knew he wasn't stalling, just trying to put something together in his head. The clock on his desk showed him that fifty-four minutes of the hour they'd been given were left.

Kreevich inhaled deeply on his cigarette and let the smoke out in a long sigh. "I've got to be rough on you, Julian. We have no guarantee that, if we turn Elissa over to the mercies of that bastard on the phone, Lydia will be set free. She knows too much. She knows who's been holding her, who his confederates are, probably what he plans to do with Elissa when he gets her. The man told us—we don't know whether she's alive now."

Quist turned away, his lower lip caught between his teeth.

"If Lydia knew what we've been ordered to do, what do you think she would say to us?" Kreevich asked.

"I think," Quist said, after a moment, "that she'd tell us we had no right to arrange for two deaths instead of one. It could mean Elissa's death as well as hers if we follow instructions."

Kreevich nodded. "A gutsy girl," he said. "I think I agree with you—which makes me more determined than ever to save her, if it isn't already too late."

"How? Go charging around at windmills?" Garvey asked.

"Withdraw from the case," Kreevich said.

"Withdraw?"

"I get Jansen to act," Kreevich said. "I get him to arrange

for the CIA, the FBI, the State Department to take Elissa out of our custody. They take her somewhere, lock her up in some high security place, and we can't turn her over to our phone pal even if we wanted to. When he calls us at the end of his hour, we are helpless. It just might give Lydia more time. Our phony Arab would have to deal with Jansen, or whoever Jansen nominates."

"Meanwhile?" Quist said.

"Meanwhile, we don't just sit here, knitting a new bedspread," Kreevich said. "I have a mass murder to deal with. We may just find something under a rock there that will point us somewhere."

"I buy it," Garvey said.

Quist sat at his desk, face buried in his hands. Finally he made a little gesture that indicated acceptance.

Part

THREE

1

Kreevich used Connie's office to make a phone call to Jansen in Washington. To Quist, Garvey, and Connie it seemed to take forever. The hour they'd been given by the accent man was slipping away.

When Kreevich rejoined them, he looked as if he'd recovered a little from his obvious fatigue.

"Done," he said. "Elissa will be moved from Dan's apartment before the hour is up." He glanced at his wristwatch and nodded. "Just about!" he added, a touch grim.

"Where will they take her?" Garvey asked.

"That has to be decided by someone else," Kreevich said. "Jansen couldn't take the time to draw up a plan. He couldn't say who would handle it till he got on the ball. But it will be done."

"Your men at Dan's apartment?" Quist asked.

"I'm on my way. You two stay here till you hear from our creep. If you're being watched, you have to look as though you're doing what you were told."

"And when he calls?"

"You've just heard from me. Federal officials have taken charge of Elissa. You'll be told to get her loose—or else."

"And—?"

"Plead for time," Kreevich said. "You don't know who's got Elissa or where they've taken her."

"The truth."

"So, you can make it sound real," Kreevich said. "I'll see you in Cuba! I may have some solid information for you next time I get in touch." He paused at the door as he was leaving. "Jansen will be able to confront Elissa with the information he has from overseas about Pat Walsh. Her answers will be interesting."

"What garbage!" Garvey said when the lieutenant had gone. "It's common gossip that Elissa made Walsh look foolish when he made a pass at her."

"Gossip spread by Walsh," Quist said. "His story. If he was trying to conceal an affair with Elissa, that would be a way to do it, wouldn't it?"

"What man wants to conceal an affair with a famous sex symbol?" Garvey asked. "He'd put it in headlines!"

"Not if he and Elissa were involved in some sort of scheme to get at Duke Maxwell and her father."

"I don't understand something," Connie said, entering herself into the conversation for the first time. "Elissa was apparently as close to her father as ham and eggs! You've both seen and heard how devastated she was by the news of his death."

"Actress," Quist said, his voice flat.

"How crazy can you be?" Garvey asked.

"Little girl who never got over knowing that her father wanted a son. Never made it with him, trying to fill that bill. Looking for a chance to get even."

"You sound like a shrink, trying to come up with a shrink-type explanation," Garvey said. "I don't buy it for a minute."

"If Jansen's information is correct, then I have to think that way," Quist said. He glanced at his watch. Five minutes to the hour.

The phone lights blinked. Connie picked up the extension and answered. "Mark," she said and handed the phone to Quist.

"Done, accomplished," Kreevich told his friend.

"Who?" Quist asked.

"Local FBI men I know. They have instructions to deliver her to Jansen. I guess they were the only people Jansen could get to in a hurry."

"How did Elissa react?" Quist asked.

"Like nothing that could happen mattered to her anymore. I would have been touched, if I hadn't found myself wondering if it was an Academy Award performance. Now, beg for time when your friend calls."

The call came almost at once, and the heavily accented voice was trembling with anger. "Just what the hell are you trying to pull off, Mr. Quist?"

"I don't understand," Quist said.

"You damn well do, Quist. You know perfectly well that Kreevich has turned Elissa over to Federal men."

"Orders from higher up," Quist said. "Kreevich didn't have the authority to overrule them. He was prepared to follow your instructions, but he had no choice."

"You don't really care about your Miss Morton, do you, Quist?"

"You know better."

"Do you have contacts anywhere that can get Elissa free?"

"I might have, but it will take time to find them and time for them to get into action."

"So move!" the voice said. "You will regret it for the rest of your life if you're playing some kind of a game with me. I'll be in touch with you, hour to hour. I don't know just how long I will let you hang me out to dry, Quist. You better be able to tell me where Elissa is, how I can verify it, and how you propose to get her out of their hands and into mine."

"I can't sit here and do it by phone," Quist said.

"Then have Garvey stay there, or your secretary. Keep in

touch with them, so they can have answers for me when I call, which will be on the hour, every hour."

"I have one thing for you," Quist said.

"Oh?"

"The next time you call, make sure it's from some place where Lydia can speak to me on the phone. Unless I know for certain that Lydia is alive and well, I'm not going to play your game any further."

"You have to be joking," the voice said. "You're not going to let your woman pay with her life for your stupidity."

"Know this," Quist said. "If you harm Lydia, if you kill her, the rest of my life will be spent hunting for you. When I find you—and I will find you sooner or later—I won't call the police. I will finish you then and there, right on the spot."

The voice broke into a short laugh. "Dreams may make you feel better, Quist. Just be certain that, if Elissa isn't very quickly in my hands, your dream will turn into a nightmare. I have no warm feeling for you or Miss Morton. I want what I want, and I mean to have it. So use every bit of influence you've got to make it come out my way—or else!"

"Like two kids exchanging threats in a school yard!" Garvey said when Quist reported the caller's threat.

"Lydia hasn't disappeared voluntarily," Quist said. "I will kill the son of a bitch when I catch up with him—if anything bad has happened to her."

"If saying that makes you feel better, fine," Garvey said. "So now what? You're not taking this Elissa-Walsh thing seriously, are you?"

"If Jansen tells me to take it seriously, I must."

"You trust him?"

"Jeremy Hoyt and Mark both trust him. I have to."

Garvey made an impatient gesture. "Let's look at some

136

certainties," he said. "If, by some farfetched possibility, Pat Walsh is involved, we have to know he isn't working alone. He's been here, he's been at my apartment, he's around. Someone else would have to be sitting on Lydia. Walsh isn't a short, chunky, blond·man—the description your elevator man gave of Bloomfield, who tapped your phone. So, Walsh or not, we are dealing with more than one person."

"Elissa could afford to hire an expensive army," Quist said.

"Elissa!" Garvey turned away, as if he was afraid he might slug his friend. "How crazy can you get, Julian? Elissa murders her father? Elissa lets herself be taken prisoner by Kreevich and then arranges to have Lydia kidnapped so you will be forced to set her free? That's padded-cell thinking, Julian."

"I have to admit that Walsh didn't sound as if he knew Elissa had escaped the bombing," Quist said.

"Of course, he didn't know! Nobody would have known, if you hadn't decided to be an honor-bright Scout and told Kreevich."

"Why do you suppose she came to us in the first place, instead of going to the police?" Quist asked.

"She needed help to get away—from the press, from Walsh, from thousands of gossip-hungry fans. You put the kibosh on that when you brought Kreevich into the picture."

"You left out one other reason she might have had for wanting to get away without letting it be known someone else had died in her place—the understudy girl. If she was meant to die, someone would still be looking for her. I was certain Kreevich was better equipped to protect her from that than you and I were. So she's safe now, with the whole damned United States government protecting her. I can't be sorry I contributed to that safety, Dan."

"It sure as hell has cost Lydia," Garvey said. The little red light blinked on the phone. "Oh come on! It isn't an hour yet."

Connie picked up the phone and answered. She turned to Quist. "Luis VanDeusen," she said.

"I know it's late, Julian," the actor said, "but I called your apartment and got no answer, so I took a chance and called your office."

"So, it's that kind of a day—or night," Quist said. "What can I do for you, Luis?"

"Is that tape still in your office, the one I heard?"

"Yes."

"Could I hear it again?"

"Sure. But why? There's nothing new on it, except more of the same."

"Could I hear what's new, too?"

"Sure, but what is all this, Luis?"

"I don't want to throw you a curve before I'm sure, Julian, but I think I heard that voice somewhere else tonight. I need to hear it again on the tape before I fire at will. A taxi will get me there in about ten minutes."

"Where, Luis? Who?"

"Please let me hear the tape again," VanDeusen said.

"I'll be here," Quist said.

He reported the gist of the conversation to Garvey and Connie.

"He thinks he heard the voice and won't tell you who it was?" Garvey asked.

"I think I can understand that," Connie said. "He wants to match the sound of the tape against what he heard somewhere else before he makes some kind of wild accusation."

VanDeusen's taxi must not have paid too much attention to the speed limit. The actor was ushered into the office by Ben, the night man, before they had stopped speculating on his call. The actor's normally ruddy complexion had been replaced by a kind of pallor.

"I was at a dinner for the Overseas Press Club," Van-
Deusen said. "I was to do a one-man act. I had to amuse the
guests. Before I was due to go on, several other people had
things to talk about. One of them did an imitation of some
Arab big shot who'd been discussed by the speaker ahead
of him. When he did the imitation, I heard the tape once
more. Let me hear it again, Julian, before I tell you who it
was."

Connie had set up the tape for playing while they'd
waited for VanDeusen, and now she started it rolling. The
now-so-familiar voice was there. "You will withdraw from
all phases of the investigation into what happened at the
Quatermayne last night. . . . you may be able to effect an
exchange. . . . Elissa Hargrove for your Miss Morton. . . .
Go to the police with this, and you can begin preparing
your lady's obituary. . . ."

The actor listened intently, his cheeks sucked in. When
the tape had run out, he sat for a moment staring at the
machine.

"Once more, that last bit," he said.

Connie rewound the tape and played it again. When it
was finished VanDeusen nodded slowly.

"The reporter who did that imitation is the same person
who made that tape," he said. "I'd swear it on my mother's
grave. It wouldn't hold up in court, of course, but he's the
man who's been talking to you. That New Yorkese, I mentioned. The whole sound of it is unmistakable."

"His name?" Quist asked, leaning forward.

"Walsh. Pat Walsh," VanDeusen said. "He's the fellow
who's been writing articles about the Hargroves, isn't he?"

"Oh, wow!" Garvey said.

"Listening to accents is my business," VanDeusen said.
"I can imitate them to a T. Let me hear a recording of
someone doing a Jewish routine or telling a Polish joke, and
I can tell you who it is if I've heard him before. Everyone
has a slightly different way of talking in an accent, their

own intonations, their own twists and quirks. Pat Walsh made that tape, Julian. As I say, it won't stand up in court, but I thought you ought to know."

Garvey was headed for the door. "Let's go!" he said.

"Hold it, Dan," Quist said, sharply. "Go where?"

"Find Walsh and beat it out of him!" Garvey said.

"Let's talk just a minute, Dan. You set this up yourself, friend. Walsh has been circulating—including this press club dinner Luis attended. So someone has to be watching Lydia. There is 'Bloomfield,' and maybe a dozen others. If Walsh doesn't check with them at specified times, they'll know something's happened to him."

"And goodbye Lydia," VanDeusen said.

"I want to get my hands on him just as badly as you do, Dan," Quist said. "But let's think very carefully about how we approach him. There has to be a right way and a dangerously wrong way."

"Turn him over to the cops," VanDeusen said. "What I have to tell them would justify an arrest."

"Like you said, Luis—'and goodbye Lydia.'"

"His life for Lydia's? That isn't a trade he would make?" Garvey asked.

"Is he just working for himself, or someone else?" Quist countered. "If he's working for terrorists, and the Quatermayne makes it look that way, he knows he will die anyway if he fails. He can't make that trade if Lydia is his one chance of getting what he wants from us—Elissa."

"So you let him win?"

"We stall, somehow, until we have an answer," Quist said.

"The answer isn't to give him a second victim by turning Elissa over to him," Garvey said.

Quist gave his friend a bitter smile. "Has it occurred to you, Dan, that Elissa may be the safest person in this whole bag of tricks? If she's the innocent victim of a terrorist attack that killed her father and her friends, just missed being killed herself, she couldn't be safer—surrounded by the police, the FBI, and Jansen's army, whoever they are. If she's a terrorist herself, involved in the deaths of forty-two people, involved with Pat Walsh, who is playing telephone games with us, then she's still safe. The police won't do anything to her without due process of law, and Walsh is no threat to her because they are partners."

"How you can go for that nonsense—"

"It has to be one or the other, Dan, and either way Elissa is safe, while Lydia—either way—is behind the biggest, blackest eight ball you ever saw. By now, she, rescued and still alive, could send Walsh and his friends up the river forever. With her, a prosecutor could nail them all. Without her, Kreevich and the rest of us will have to come up with an airtight case, evidence that will convince a jury. If I can't sell you, Dan, what chance is there to sell a skeptical jury? Elissa is a folk heroine, every man's dream of romance."

"Not to the women on the jury," Connie said. "They'd probably be just as prejudiced the other way."

"So we leave the legal aspects of it to Kreevich and the FBI and Karl Jansen, whoever he is. We go illegal, locate Lydia, and chop Mr. Pat Walsh into very small pieces," Garvey said.

"If it isn't already too late," Quist said.

2

Words and words and words and words. You could talk about it, Quist thought, and guess about it, but what could they *do* about it? Garvey had said "Let's go!" But where? Walsh had them over a barrel. In this city of millions, Lydia was a very small needle in a monstrous haystack. You couldn't walk out of this office and head for any place specific. The best possible bet, of course, was to put a tail on Walsh, wait for him to go to where Lydia was being held. Neither Quist nor Dan could be effective at that. Walsh would spot them, no matter what kind of attempt at disguise they used. All Walsh had to do was recognize that someone was appearing a little too often wherever he went. He'd guess, then, that someone was on to him. Wouldn't that produce an instant order for the elimination of Lydia?

"I'm not accustomed to this sort of game," Luis Van-Deusen said, breaking a heavy silence, "except as I've come across it in radio, film, and TV scripts. This one is wilder than most, and if I read it in a script, I'd think it was impossible to sell."

"But you'd try to sell it, doubts or not," Quist said. "That's what you get paid for."

"Selling it is precisely what I was going to suggest," the actor said. "Tell me to shut up, if you want."

"About all we can do, Luis, is to listen," Quist said, "no matter how wild the idea."

VanDeusen leaned forward in his chair, eyes bright. "Motive for all of this, Julian? It has to be money and power, doesn't it?"

"Or Walsh is trying just as hard as I am to free his woman," Quist said.

"Isn't that chapter two in his script?" VanDeusen asked. "Chapter one was the massacre of forty-two innocent people, among them enemies of Walsh's, wasn't it. But in the process Elissa fell into the hands of the police. Kidnapping Lydia was a way to free her."

"So?"

"From what I've heard, Julian, they were involved in some kind of scam, some kind of power-and-money grab in the Middle East."

"A guess," Quist said. "You might call the Middle East their home ball park."

"So they have friends there with money and power. They also have enemies."

"Months to separate the sheep from the goats," Garvey said.

"Maybe not," VanDeusen said. "Do you have any idea how to reach Walsh on the telephone?"

"He's not listed in the book," Connie said. "I've already checked."

"The news syndicate he works for?" Quist suggested.

"Pretty sketchy touchdowns there, I imagine," Van-Deusen said. "But they would know how to reach him."

"So, for the sake of argument, we've got him."

VanDeusen took a deep breath. What came from him was startling, a deep voice, heavily accented. "I think you will know who I am, Mr. Walsh. We cannot allow you to use Miss Morton as a hostage. It can bring down the United States Navy, Marines, and covert CIA agents on our heads. Turn her loose! Elissa Hargrove can buy or bargain her way

143

out of trouble." VanDeusen let his breath out in a long sigh. "How do you like it?" he asked, in his normal voice.

"Oh, brother!" Garvey said.

"Marvelous, but so what?" Quist said.

"You are dealing with a man, Walsh, who understands terrorism and how it works," VanDeusen said. "Would he doubt for a minute, if he talks to that person I just invented, that counterforces who will stop at nothing have gotten involved? He has thrown you a curve with a phony Arab. I can throw him one back with another."

"It just might be he would buy it," Quist said, after a moment. "He'd check and double-check, though—where the call came from. It couldn't be a fake overseas operator; he could check it out."

"It wouldn't have to come from overseas," VanDeusen said. "Not with the United Nations just around the corner. There are plenty of strong-arm guys there, posing as peacemakers. A street-corner pay phone. No way he could trace it."

"It wouldn't work," Garvey said. "It might just hurry him into harming Lydia."

"His phony Arab has worked with you, hasn't it?" Van-Deusen asked. "Mine could work with him. Incidentally, that voice I used is a copy of Colonel Khadafy, the Libyan strong man. I used it in a film."

"It's a gamble," Quist said, "one I'm not sure I want to take. It could free Lydia; it could cut her chances off."

"It could make Walsh hesitate, give you a little time," VanDeusen suggested.

You hold a match near the gunpowder, and you have to be an expert to know just how close you can get without setting off the charge. What would Walsh's reaction be to a threat from an unknown Arab enemy? Would he decide it was too dangerous for him to ignore a warning, or too dangerous for him not to?

144

"If Walsh guesses that we've guessed—"

"What can we lose?" Garvey asked. "He deals with us direct, instead of all these comic opera dialects. We still can meet his demands, or we can't. He holds the top card, one way or the other."

"It's just possible he would buy what I try to sell him," VanDeusen said.

"I think—I think it's worth a try," Quist said.

The minute he'd made the decision, Quist doubted the wisdom of it. There was time to change his mind at the last minute. It wasn't going to be easy to locate Walsh, get set up so that he would answer a call from an untraceable number. There would be time to locate Kreevich and ask his advice. There would be time to say "no" at the last minute. Still, they were doing something, which was a relief.

VanDeusen and Garvey had gone out to find a phone that could be used in the hoax on Walsh. Connie was calling the news syndicate, to try to get a number from them where Walsh could be reached. Walsh had covered himself. The syndicate wouldn't give out a number, but they would reach Walsh and give him a number he could call.

"I'll get back to you," was all Connie could say until VanDeusen and Garvey checked back.

Quist was on another phone, trying to locate Kreevich. At headquarters he finally caught up with Sergeant Adams, one of Kreevich's men who knew that Quist was a genuine friend.

"He's been on the job for damn near a day and a half, Mr. Quist. He had to get some shut-eye or collapse."

"He's at home?"

"Phone off the hook, unless he's out of his mind," Adams said.

Kreevich's apartment was down in the Village, not too

far from Center Street Police Headquarters. Quist tried the lieutenant's number and got a busy signal—endlessly. Adams was right: the phone was off the hook.

"I've got to talk to him, Connie," Quist said.

"What about Walsh?"

"When Dan and Luis have a number set up for him to call, hold the fort," Quist said. "I'll call you back, as soon as I've talked to Mark."

The ride downtown in a taxi seemed to take forever. The old brownstone house where Kreevich had his apartment looked dark, except for a light in the front hall. People had gone to bed. It was going on midnight.

Quist pressed the button under Kreevich's name in the lobby. Nothing. He kept at it, two or three shorts, a long, more shorts. "All night if I have to, pal," he said under his breath. Finally Kreevich's voice, sleep clouded, came over the intercom.

"You out of your mind, or something?"

"I'm sorry, Mark. It's Julian, and it's vital."

The lock release sounded, and Quist walked into the house. Kreevich's apartment was on the second floor, and the detective was waiting for Quist when he got there.

"I can't say I'm tickled to death to see you, Julian," he muttered. He was wearing a navy blue summer robe and his feet were bare. "Twenty-eight straight hours. I had to get something, chum."

"I have something," Quist said. Inside the living room, curtains blowing gently at the windows, he told his friend about VanDeusen and the actor's positive identification of the accented voice of Lydia's kidnapper.

"It will help when the right time comes," Kreevich said, "but I haven't been waiting for it. Ever since Karl Jansen gave me the word on Walsh and Elissa Hargrove, I've had a tail on him. He's like a water bug, all over the place. When I turned in, he was at his apartment, apparently shacked up for the night."

"You haven't picked him up? Lydia could be in that apartment of his."

"No way. Walsh knows that we might want to question him—about Elissa, of course. We'd go to his apartment to find him. No way he'd be holding a prisoner there."

Quist told him about his scheme for throwing a scare into Walsh. Kreevich listened, frowning.

"If your actor friend is as good as you say, he could throw a scare into Walsh. But with what results? He could take a powder; he could order Lydia's elimination at once. She knows too much. He could rally his army around him and hole up somewhere, after contacting his friends in the Middle East to find out who the hell is threatening him."

"But, if you have him covered, wherever he holes up, you'd be there—if your people are any good," Quist said.

"The best," Kreevich said.

"So do we try it, or do we just wait somewhere and sweat?" Quist asked.

Kreevich's smile was weary. "You don't have much sweat left to sweat, do you, chum?"

"Not much. Any kind of action—"

Kreevich took a deep breath. "Let me give you the hard core, Julian—and I hate to do it."

"You don't think we're going to get Lydia back?"

"Unhappily—I don't think so."

"Not even if you turned Elissa over to him?"

"Specially not then," Kreevich said. "He and Elissa could take off for the moon then, and they wouldn't leave Lydia alive to tell what she knows."

"You're certain they are lovers—in spite of all Walsh's columns and attacks on the Hargroves?"

"Jansen's people are certain. Lydia may live, as long as she can be used to persuade us to free Elissa. Once she's served her purpose—goodnight, sweet princess."

"Oh God, Mark!"

"Should you go ahead with VanDeusen's trick? I can only

147

say this—and I don't mean it as advice. It could throw Walsh off balance for a moment or two. He might just make a move that would give us a lead to wherever Lydia may be—a phone call, a quick move away from his apartment to somewhere else."

"What good would a phone call do us?"

"I'm not dead yet, Julian. He's got an unlisted number, but I have it covered, a man listening round the clock. I can give you that number, VanDeusen can call him there, and we can wait and see—and hope."

"If you were me, would you risk that, Mark?"

"If I were you—I don't know what I'd do, Julian. But I am me, and as a cop I would take the chance, because it just may be the only thing that will give Lydia a hope."

"Give me that unlisted number," Quist said.

Dan Garvey and Luis VanDeusen had, in effect, taken over a public phone booth on First Avenue and were waiting there for a green light from Quist.

"Kreevich approves," Quist told Garvey when he reached his friend at the number that had been left with Connie. "What I have for you from Mark is Walsh's unlisted phone. It's being monitored, so whoever is listening in will know what's really happening."

"What does Kreevich think Walsh will do?" Dan asked.

"Walsh just might let his foot slip an inch," Quist said. "He's certain Lydia isn't being held at Walsh's apartment. Too much traffic there. But Walsh is also being tailed. If he goes somewhere, or calls somewhere, we just might have a lead."

"Luis's ready if you say so," Garvey said.

"Go," Quist said and felt a cold chill run along his spine. A long shot, but the only shot. He reached out his hand, felt something hot, and saw that Connie had supplied him with a mug of coffee.

"It will work, Julian," she said. "It has to."

He looked at her, his eyelids heavy. "You read and hear every day about some bloody violence," he said, "but it isn't going to happen to you, not ever. So here it is!"

"Mark Kreevich is so very much on the ball, Julian. If anyone can bring Walsh to heel, he's it."

"I don't have any doubts that Kreevich and his contacts will make Walsh and Elissa pay for what they've done," Quist said. "But it's always been Mark's complaint that he never gets into the picture till after the crime has been committed. Forty-two people bombed at the Quatermayne, but Mark doesn't get into the act till they're all dead. Now there's Lydia!"

"It won't be, Julian. It can't be."

"Innocent bystander," Quist said. "It's always the innocent bystander who gets creamed." He glanced at his watch. "How long is it since we've heard from Walsh's Arab phony? More than an hour, and he said every hour on the hour."

"He has to sleep, like anyone else, like you should," Connie said.

"You don't really believe I could, do you?" he asked. "And Walsh won't be asleep now, if Dan and Luis are doing their thing."

"Will he guess it's not real, do you think?"

Quist shrugged. "There's too much we don't understand yet to know," he said. "Why the wholesale slaughter at the Quatermayne? Some kind of revenge? Some kind of cover-up? It wasn't just an angry man running wild. Three bombs, carefully planted—a time-consuming job—set to go off at an exact moment."

"But so many innocent people involved only with the theater project," Connie said.

"Among those people, there must have been one or two or more who could have supported Duke Maxwell when he lowered the boom on Elissa and Walsh. They couldn't pick them off, one by one, and since they were all under the same roof—to hell with the innocent bystanders."

"Walsh knows that Elissa is alive?"

"Of course! They planned it all together."

"The doctor who treated Elissa for laryngitis?"

"Want to bet that there never was a doctor?" Quist asked. "The stage manager who is supposed to have sent him is dead. There was never a doctor, and that's why no doctor will come forward and say that he treated Elissa for anything."

"All a fake?"

"Everything about this mess is a fake—except Lydia," Quist said. "Walsh's harrassment of Elissa in the press was a fake. They are lovers. Elissa's grief over her father's death is a fake. She had a lifelong hatred for him, for wanting a son instead of her. She tried to be a son by working in her father's business, learning the technology, Beth Storrs told us. Has it occurred to you that she had the skills to set up those bombs in the Quatermayne? She would have been free to wander anywhere in the theater she wanted to. No one would have questioned her, and no one is left alive now to give it a second thought."

"Except Guardino, the man who went for coffee," Connie said.

"Either he didn't see her, or he is one of them," Quist said. "It goes on and on, like a gory soap opera. Duke Maxwell wasn't what he appeared to be—a highly successful promoter of sports. Actually an undercover operator for the government. Jansen was right. You have to guess no one is what they appear to be."

"Except Elissa. She is a real movie star."

"And that reality is a cover for what?" Quist asked. "She escaped the bomb with a reasonable story to explain how and why. All she had to do was come forward, in public, and make the press and all her fans happy. Instead, she tries me and then Dan, expecting us to keep it a secret. Why? So she could 'grieve' in private over her father's death? I don't think so."

"Then why, Julian?"

"I don't know yet—maybe Jansen does—what she and Walsh were up to. Probably some big deal with enemy Arab powers in the Middle East—selling Hargrove weapons to the enemy. It could involve millions of dollars, probably salted away in a Swiss bank account. They had to get to their money without attracting attention. Dan and I, a couple of suckers, would help her disappear. Walsh could come and go, they thought, but she couldn't walk out the door without being held up forever by the cops, the press. We, she thought, because of our soft hearts, would help her get away. I turned out to be sticky, by informing Kreevich. And so—Lydia. Now they have to play hard ball."

The phone blinked. Connie answered it.

"Dan," she said and handed the instrument to Quist.

"It's done," Garvey told Quist. "We recorded it. We're on our way to you so you can hear it."

"How did he take it?"

"The way you'd expect," Garvey said. "He didn't know what the hell we were talking about. But he knew, and he knows someone has the whole story on him from top to bottom. I hope to God Kreevich's people stay close to him. His next move could be to make sure Lydia never gets to talk. We're on our way. If you want Kreevich to hear it—?"

"I'll call him. Step on it, Dan."

"We're not ten minutes away," Garvey said.

It was as if each tick of the clock on Quist's desk rang a gong in his ears. Kreevich sounded cool on the phone. The man monitoring Walsh's phone had already reported.

"Your actor fellow evidently did a hell of a job," the detective said. "We waited for Walsh to make a call to someone after it was over, but he didn't. He's not a dummy. Your actor called him on his unlisted phone. He has to have guessed that phone isn't safe. I think he'll deliver his orders from an outside phone, or carry them out himself."

"He won't be able to slip the tail you've got on him?"

"Not unless he can take off into space," Kreevich said. "I'll listen to the recording later, Julian. Right now I'm going to stay here till someone reports something positive."

"If he tries to use a public phone?"

"We'll stall him somehow," Kreevich said. "Keep in touch, if your actor friend can add anything to what we've already heard."

Eight minutes had clicked off on the clock when Dan and VanDeusen walked into the office. Neither one of them looked too happy.

"Maybe all we did was warn him that someone knew what was up," Garvey said.

"That's for sure," VanDeusen said. "But, if he has Arab enemies, he could have believed I was who I pretended to be." He put a little tape recorder down on Quist's desk. "This may not be the best recording ever. We had to hold the mike right next to the ear piece. It may have missed a thing or two from him. My voice will sound extra loud."

"Play it," Quist said.

There was a scratchy sound that Quist recognized as a number being dialed on a phone. Then the sound of a ringing—five times before a disgruntled voice answered.

"Pat Walsh here."

"You may recognize my voice, Walsh." It was Luis's "Colonel Khadafy." "If you don't, you will know who I represent."

"I don't recognize your voice. Who do you represent?"

"Let's not waste time, Walsh," the Arab voice said. "You are holding Miss Lydia Morton, Julian Quist's lady, hostage, demanding that Elissa Hargrove be set free."

"Elissa Hargrove is dead. What are you talking about?"

"You know what I'm talking about, Walsh. My people

cannot allow you to play this game. Harm Miss Morton, and all the forces of the United States government will be down on us. So I warn you—set Miss Morton free and unharmed at once, or I promise you that you and Miss Hargrove will not live to enjoy the future you have planned."

"You're off your rocker," Walsh said. "I don't know anything about Miss Morton. As far as I know, Miss Hargrove died in the bombing last night. Whoever you are, somebody has given you a very bum steer."

"Play it the way you choose, Walsh. But this is no joke. Add up the consequences to us if you persist in this, and you will understand why you and Miss Hargrove will be exposed and destroyed. We don't make hollow threats, Walsh, and you very well know it."

"How did you get this unlisted number?"

The Arab voice laughed. "You don't think there's any problem to getting your number when we wanted it. You haven't much time, Walsh, if your twisted world isn't about to come to an end."

"You are crazy, no matter who you are," Walsh said.

"Goodbye, Walsh," the Arab voice said, and there was the sound of the dial tone.

VanDeusen was mopping at his face with a handkerchief as he shut off the recorder. "Maybe I wasn't as good as I thought," he said. "It didn't seem to shake him up at all."

"Maybe he's as good as Elissa at theatrics," Garvey said.

"So what have we accomplished, except to tell him that we know what he's up to?" Garvey asked.

"Knowing that, he has to act," Quist said. "Let's hope Kreevich's men are as good as he thinks they are."

The red phone light blinked again. Every hour on the hour? Connie held the instrument out to Quist. "Lieutenant Kreevich," she said.

"Hold onto your hat, Julian," the detective said. "Walsh

left his apartment very shortly after the phone call. My men followed him. At this moment he has just entered the lobby of your office building, presumably on the way to see you. Play it cool, friend. We're not going to find Lydia unless he makes a mistake."

Quist reported to the others. "Luis, you wait in Connie's office. If he sees you, he'll recognize you from the press club dinner. Dan and Connie belong here."

The actor picked up the recorder and scurried into Connie's office. Almost at the same moment Ben, the night man, was at the main office door.

"Pat Walsh is here again," he said.

"Show him in, Ben."

Walsh showed no signs of strain as he breezed into the office. "I tried you at home," he said to Quist. "No answer, so I took a chance you might be here. Don't you ever go to bed?"

"Like you, I have to watch the stew while it's cooking," Quist said.

The impulse to charge the man, standing there, smiling, was almost irresistible. Charge him, strangle the truth out of him—beat the life out of him if necessary. One slender thread of sanity held Quist back. Someone had said, or had he thought it himself, that, if Walsh didn't report on a regular basis to whoever was guarding Lydia, there could be standing instructions on how to deal with her.

"Your stew is a little more complicated than you lead me to believe, isn't it, Quist? Ingredients in it you weren't willing to tell me about?"

Had those slender, strong-looking hands touched Lydia? Had that sardonic smile accompanied threats Walsh had made to her? Had he been the one who forced her to write the note for the phony Bloomfield? Later—when Lydia was free—he would track this bastard to the ends of the earth.

"It's been a long, hard day, Walsh. What is it now?" Quist asked.

"You knew when I was here before, didn't you?" Walsh said. "You knew that Elissa was alive." There was something deadly about the voice gone suddenly so cold.

"Alive?" Quist struggled to make it sound real.

"There's always somebody who will leak like a broken faucet," Walsh said. "Policemen don't get paid enough, do they? How does the old saying go? 'Visions of sugarplums dance in their eyes'? Buying information from cops is an old story in my business." He turned to look at Garvey. "I had to find out what was going on at your apartment, Garvey, and I finally found the leaky faucet. Elissa was there, wasn't she?"

Garvey gave him a look of elaborate innocence. "Where's my sugarplum?" he asked.

"Could we cut all this crap out?" Walsh said. "She was there at your apartment, Dan, and you were with her. You, too, Quist. And the noble lieutenant from Homicide was with her for a couple of hours. What's it all about?"

"If you know all this, why don't you print it?" Quist asked. "It would be the scoop of all time, wouldn't it? Elissa Hargrove alive and well and living in Dan Garvey's apartment."

"Because the cops will deny it, you two jerks will deny it, and my leaky faucet will dry up," Walsh said.

"Did your 'leaky faucet' tell you how Elissa escaped the bombing?" Quist asked.

"A piece of bad luck that turned out to be a godsend. You know how as well as I do. She lost her voice, couldn't go on, and her understudy died in her place. I want to know two things. Why are the police keeping this a secret, and where are they holding her?"

"You would print that if we told you?" Quist asked.

"Of course I would—and will, when it breaks."

"Why come to us? Why not to Kreevich?"

"I owe something to the guy who spilled the beans," Walsh said. "But I don't owe anything to you, or to little

Miss Muffet over there." He nodded toward Connie.

"You could do an 'I am lead to believe' piece," Garvey said.

"I am never 'lead to believe.' I print what I know. Where is Kreevich? I haven't been able to find him."

"Didn't your 'leaky faucet' tell you where he lives and what his private phone number is?" Garvey asked.

Now, Quist thought, is the time to grab him, to pound the truth out of him. Behind that sour smile of his was the answer to Lydia's safety. He sat straight and still behind his desk, gripping the arms of his desk chair. Play it cool, friend.

"So you know that Elissa is alive," he said very quietly. "You also know, if you give it a second's thought, why Kreevich hasn't told the world. He has a massacre to solve, and Elissa may still be a target for terror. Naturally he'll keep her safe. Naturally he doesn't want you or any other reporters spreading the news. It could be dangerous for Elissa, and it would inform the terrorists that they still have to make another move."

"So where is he holding her?" Walsh demanded.

"I don't have the answer to that," Quist said, "and you can give me a lie detector test on that. Didn't your 'faucet' tell you that Federal agents took Elissa away from Dan's apartment."

"Yes, he did. I didn't believe it at first. Is she here in New York? Have they taken her somewhere out of town?"

"With all your 'sugarplums,' you ought to be able to find that out for yourself," Garvey said. "From what you say, there must be 'leaky faucets' in other places."

"How did she happen to wind up in your apartment, Garvey?"

"She came to us for help," Garvey said. "She couldn't locate Julian, so she came to me. She didn't want people to know she'd escaped until she was sure she was safe. We decided the police could give her the best possible protection, so we called in Kreevich, who is a friend."

Would it come now? A threat, a veiled threat? The mistake they were hoping for? Almost, but not quite.

"I will remember, someday, that you two wouldn't cooperate with me when I needed it," Walsh said. He turned and left.

Garvey started after him and stopped when he reached the door. "If he catches sight of me following him, we've had it," he said, pounding a fist against the wall. "We have to leave it to Kreevich's men. If one of them is a bad apple, they may lose him."

Quist was already dialing Kreevich's number. He described Walsh's visit to the detective.

"No way one of my men was bought off," Kreevich said. "He knew that Elissa was alive, because it was all planned in advance between them. They counted on you and Dan, nice, kindly, softhearted gents, to get her away without anyone knowing. You were smart enough to know she'd be safer with me."

"I don't give a damn about her safety," Quist said. "You have no idea what it was like, Mark, having him stand here, not three feet away, and let him walk out of here with Lydia's life in his hands."

"I can arrest them both, hold them forever," Kreevich said, "and we'll be looking for Lydia at the bottom of the East River. Sit tight, Julian, and keep your phone line open. I'm guessing you'll be hearing from your Arab voice again, as soon as Walsh can get to a safe phone."

"If your men heard him pulling that accent job on me, would they take him in?"

"Not without a 'yes' from me," Kreevich said. "When I give them a go ahead, it will be because I'm convinced there's no chance for Lydia.

"When he calls, insist on being given some proof that

she's all in one piece. So much time has gone by, he must know you have doubts. It might work. Meanwhile, I'll try to set up something that will help."

"Like what?"

"Clear your line, Julian. Play for time. Get some reassurance if you can."

3

It was almost as if Kreevich had had an advance look at the script. VanDeusen had come back in from Connie's office, and he was saying that, for certain, Walsh was the man who'd been faking the Arab accent. Listening to him speak normally to Julian had only reinforced that conviction.

The phone light blinked. Connie answered, and the look on her face made words unnecessary. The Arab voice was on again. It hadn't taken Walsh long to find what he thought was a safe phone.

Quist wigwagged directions. VanDeusen was to listen on the extension, Connie was to turn on the recorder. He picked up his own phone.

"Julian Quist here," he said.

"You're not being very clever about this, Mr. Quist," the deep Arab voice said. Across the room VanDeusen nodded vigorously.

"You haven't called when you said you would," Quist said.

"Because I've been waiting for you to take some kind of action, Quist," the voice said. "I'm running out of time."

"I'm doing the best I can," Quist said. "I've arranged for a meeting with Kreevich. I may be able to persuade him to tell me where they are holding Elissa. What I can do if I find that out, I don't know."

"If you find that out and you tell me the truth, it may help," the voice said.

159

"You're asking me to betray a friend, to betray my own government," Quist said. "I can't do that without some reassurance from you. Prove to me that Lydia is alive. Without that I have to throw in the towel."

There was a long hesitation, and then the Arab voice, Walsh's Arab, spoke again. "Wait ten minutes for a call, Quist. After that I give you a couple of hours to find out what I have to know, and what you plan to do about it."

"Let us pray," VanDeusen said, as the phones were put down. "No question about the voice. It's Walsh."

It was the longest ten minutes Quist could ever remember. The phone light blinked, and Quist reached for the instrument. He had come to hate the phone in the last hours, but this time he was eager.

"Julian?" It was Lydia's voice.

"Oh, my darling, are you all right?"

"Physically—all right, Julian."

"Where are you?"

"In a room."

"Where?"

"Julian, standing almost close enough to me for me to touch him is a man with a gun pointed at my head. I know he has orders to use it if I tell you anything but that I'm still all in one piece."

"Is the man someone I know?"

"No."

"Pat Walsh?"

"No."

"Do you know what they're demanding of me?"

"Yes. I'm afraid this is all the time they're giving me, Julian. I'm being told to hang up."

"Lydia! You know I'll do what I can. You know I love you, love you."

"Thanks for that. I got you into this by being the biggest sucker of all time. I'm sorry. I—"

The phone was obviously taken away from her, and the

inevitable dial tone sounded in his ear. He stood where he was, frozen.

"She's alive?" Garvey asked.

Quist nodded. "Alive—for now."

The perpetual light blinked on the phone again. Quist didn't wait for Connie. It was Walsh, the Arab Walsh.

"You satisfied, Quist?"

"Thanks for that little," Quist said.

"It's gained you two hours, Quist. I'll call you back at three this morning. If you don't have answers for me then, we're through dealing. It's your choice to make. You may not live comfortably, knowing that you refused to do anything for your Miss Morton."

Once more the dial tone. Quist thought he might never live again without hearing it going on and on. He called Kreevich, reaching him finally at the Hotel Beaumont.

"It worked," he told his friend. "Lydia is alive. She talked to me. I said I was on my way to see you. What now, Mark? What the hell now?"

"She couldn't give you a clue as to where she is?"

"Of course not. Man holding a gun on her. If she'd tried, I'd have heard her die!"

"You've been given time?"

"Two hours."

Kreevich sounded decisive. "Come over to the Beaumont. It's only a couple of blocks from where you are. The security man there is named Dodd. He'll be expecting you and bring you to where I'll be. Two hours isn't much time."

Quist relayed all that to Garvey and Connie and Van-Deusen. "Stay here," he said. "Take the call if I'm not back here at three o'clock. Stall him somehow, but don't tell him where I am."

"Be back," Garvey said, his voice grim. "I don't trust myself to handle that bastard!"

* * *

161

The Beaumont is New York's top luxury hotel. It was, as Kreevich had said, just three blocks up Park Avenue from Quist's office. The city was quiet as he walked up the avenue, the sky dotted with stars, a slim new moon in the sky to the west. It was somehow an unlikely setting for nightmares.

In the lobby of the Beaumont, a wiry little man with very bright blue eyes accosted Quist.

"I'm Jerry Dodd, Mr. Quist," he said. "Know you by sight. You and Miss Morton have been here often."

It was true. Quist and Lydia had often stopped here for a drink in the Trapeze Bar, spent some pleasant evenings in the Blue Lagoon night club. Wonderful food, expert service, friendly faces.

"Lieutenant Kreevich is waiting for you in one of the private rooms in the east wing," Dodd said. "Follow me."

The private rooms were reserved for banquets, board meetings of big corporations, small weddings, special occasions of all sorts. The room would be furnished according to the purpose for which it was being used.

Dodd led Quist down a corridor off the lobby. That lobby was busy with people still out on the town at one o'clock in the morning. Quist could hear music coming from the Blue Lagoon. It seemed like an odd place for Kreevich to choose for a meeting. It was too busy. Quist expected to run into people he knew, be bombarded with questions about the tragedy at the Quatermayne. Fortunately people were heading in another direction from the hallway down which Dodd led him.

A uniformed cop stood outside a closed door. He nodded to Dodd, opened the door, and let him in.

The large room was almost bare of furniture. There was a large stretcher table with half a dozen Windsor chairs set around it. There was a silver thermos jug on the table surrounded by coffee cups, which nobody seemed to have used. There was a telephone on the table. This, Quist found himself thinking, was a saga about telephones. But he wasn't really thinking; he was focused on the people who sat around the table. Kreevich sat there, looking like the man who had just taken the cover off a tomato surprise—pleased with himself. Fred Vail, Duke Maxwell's lawyer was there. There was also a distinguished-looking, gray-haired man Quist didn't know, and a policeman sitting in front of a stenotype machine. These were almost like dream figures in the background for Quist. He found himself riveted on the person who sat in the chair at the head of the table. It was Elissa Hargrove, looking beautiful and angry.

"I guess I have you to thank for this, Julian," she said. Her almost musical voice sounded perfectly normal, no trace of the harshness that had afflicted it the last time they'd talked. "Your friends seem to be willing to try anything to make themselves smell sweet in high places."

Quist glanced at Kreevich.

"Gloves-off time," the detective said. "You haven't met Karl Jansen."

The gray-haired man nodded. "We've talked on the phone, Mr. Quist."

"Why are we here at the Beaumont?" Quist asked.

"Hub of the wheel," Kreevich answered. "Your office and apartment, Dan's apartment, Pat Walsh's apartment—all within a very few blocks. We can move wherever we choose to go in no time."

"Gloves off, you said?"

"We've been playing the game Miss Hargrove's way for too long," the detective said. "Now she's going to have to play it our way. Lovely speaking voice, don't you think?"

"Laryngitis isn't a life sentence," Elissa said. "I couldn't go on last night. Tonight I could have gone on—if there'd been anything to go on with."

"I think we'd have to say that's only one count in the indictment against you, Miss Hargrove," Jansen said, in a pleasant, Harvard-tinged voice.

"You have questioned me and questioned me till I'm dead on my feet," Elissa said. "You've flown me to Washington and back. I'm entitled to legal counsel, and you haven't let me get to a lawyer."

"There's a way you can get yourself a lawyer in five minutes," Kreevich said.

"How?"

"Pick up that phone, call Pat Walsh, and tell him to deliver Lydia Morton here, safe and unharmed. And when she's here, you can hire yourself the whole bar association. I suspect you can afford it."

"You think I'm my father's heir?" Elissa asked.

"If you are, the court won't let you collect, Miss H. Murder for profit isn't recognized by the courts. I was thinking of your private bank account. Where is it? Switzerland? Libya?"

"That is the kind of malarkey these people have been aiming at me, Julian," Elissa said. "What is this about Lydia Morton?"

"I'm tired, too, Miss Hargrove, from having you throw your malarkey at us," Jansen said.

"Ask them to make sense, Julian!" Elissa said.

"Lydia has been kidnapped," Quist said. "The price for her release is to turn you over to Pat Walsh."

"That sounds like him, the jerk! He's been gunning for me forever. You're saying he has kidnapped Miss Morton?"

"Was Walsh gunning for you the nights you spent together in the Chateau Fontaineau in Paris?" Jansen asked.

"Nights I spent with him—?"

"Or the nights you spent with him in Hassam Rhamad's villa in Beirut?" Jansen said, sounding bored.

"Or in your house in Hollywood a couple of months ago?" Kreevich added.

"Walsh is my enemy!" Elissa protested. "It's on the re-cord! It's been in his syndicated column for the last two years!"

"It's too late, Miss Hargrove," Jansen said. "It kept us blinded for a long time, but it's over. It would save time, you know, if you would tell us the story, instead of having us tell it to you."

"'Story' is the right word for it," Elissa said. "I spent time in some kind of love affair with a man I hate? Was I selling my body to get some kind of evidence for my father?"

"You were keeping an affair with Walsh secret, and Walsh was pretending to be your enemy, so that you could destroy your father," Jansen said.

"Time," Quist said, sounding desperate. "I have an hour and a half."

"Okay. So let's take it from the top, Jansen," Kreevich said.

The gray-haired man nodded. "From the very top," he said. "Let's go back twenty years, when you were seven years old, Miss Hargrove, when you started to hate your father because he had wanted a son so badly. Was it then that you determined to pay him back in spades for not wanting you? Even as a kid you knew that before you in his affections came his industrial empire. Do something to damage that, and you could hit him where it really hurt."

"What nonsense! I loved my father. He took me everywhere with him. There wasn't a day of my life that he didn't give me my own personal time with him, his per-sonal attention."

"Oh, I'm sure he loved you. But you weren't the son he could leave his empire to. In your teens, you worked in one of his plants, didn't you?"

"Of course. I wanted to know all the details of his busi-ness, so I could share with him what pleased him."

"So you could use what you learned to hurt him," Jansen said.

"Oh, please, Mr. Jansen, do we have to go on with this nonsense?"

"From the top, right on down to the finish," Jansen said. He took a cigarette from a silver case and lit it. "That's where you learned about the technology of modern weapons, wasn't it, Miss Hargrove? Did you learn, while you worked there in your summer vacations as a teenager, how to rig explosives? No matter, because up to now I'm just conjecturing."

"Dreaming is more like it," Elissa said.

"So, now we will deal with facts. You must have guessed, Miss Hargrove, that I have long been involved with espionage in the Middle East. That's been my job, my expertise. A couple of years ago we were led to believe, through sources we trusted, that your father was involved in huge deals with enemy countries, supplying weapons to them that were used against our friends and our own troops. We began to work at it. We had a man whom we thought your father would never suspect, Duke Maxwell, the big sports promoter. Maxwell traveled all over the world with his promotions, and he was enormously helpful to us. He had a game he could play with the rich and the powerful without being suspected of being anything but a—a salesman of entertainment. He began to work on your father. None of us dreamed back then that you, now a famous movie star, could be in any way involved."

"That was before you went insane," Elissa said.

"That was before a friend of yours broke down and supplied us with the facts to save his own neck," Jansen said.

"I don't have any friends with necks that need saving!"

"I'm referring, of course, to Hassam Rhamad, the Arab wheeler and dealer, who has a villa in Beirut, a house in Tripoli, a third in Khomeini's backyard, in Iran. He professes to represent powerful oil interests, when, in fact, he's a negotiator and dealer in weapons and high technology, which he buys under the table and sells to revolutionaries and terrorists. You and your father knew him well, were guests in his various houses, and he actually loaned you the Beirut villa last summer. That's when you spent ten days there with Pat Walsh, your lover."

"That last is absolutely false," Elissa said. "Pat Walsh, my lover? That's too much, Mr. Jansen. Yes, I know Hassam Rhamad. Yes, he had, I supposed, business dealings with my father. Yes, we dined at his homes. But I never spent ten days at his Beirut place with Pat Walsh or anyone else."

Jansen reached out for the black leather briefcase on the table beside him, opened it, and took out what appeared to be several eight by ten photographs. "Rhamad had to be covered in case the roof fell in on him," he said. He slid the pictures across the tabletop to Elissa. "Don't get ideas, Miss Hargrove. Copies of these and the negatives are on file. You see there—the top one—a nude frolic in Rhamad's pool—you and Walsh; a breakfast on the terrace in a night-robe and pajamas—you and Walsh; a passionate embrace under a palm tree in the garden—you and Walsh. You weren't acting for a film, Miss Hargrove, but it came out on film, because Rhamad needed something he could use in case you decided to double-cross him."

Quist couldn't see the photographs from where he stood, but the frozen look on Elissa's pale face was all he needed.

"We knew, from evidence our agents had collected," Jansen went on, "that the revolutionary and terrorist groups with whom Rhamad dealt were in possession of sophisticated weapons and nuclear technology that could only have come from Hargrove Arms. No one else makes them! We naturally assumed that your father was dealing with the enemy. That's when Duke Maxwell was put on him."

After a moment of silence Kreevich broke in. "You don't seem surprised, Miss Hargrove."

Nothing from Elissa.

"Maxwell began sifting and sifting what came his way," Jansen continued. "He got to know your father well, involved him in sports, which he loved. The deeper he got into it the more certain Duke's doubts became that your father was the villain in the piece. He was certain it had to be someone else in Hargrove Arms who was selling us out. Duke finally laid it on the table for your father. At first your father insisted that no one person could have divulged the secrets of his company. Security and secrecy in the manufacture of weaponry was such that no one man knew every step in any one process. The technical secrets had been developed over a period of years, and only one man knew them all—your father himself. As for completed weapons, they were only shipped out with approval from the front office—your father's office, Miss Hargrove. Still Duke believed in him."

"Even when shipping orders were signed by your father, Elissa," Fred Vail, the lawyer, said, speaking for the first time. "I was the first suspect. I supervised all the contracts your father signed. Only I, it appeared, could have betrayed him."

"So why did you?" Elissa asked.

"I didn't," Vail said. "I got lucky for the first time. The second time was last night, when I wasn't in reach of the bombs in the Quatermayne. The first time I got pneumonia, was in the hospital in Paris for ten days. In that time several key orders went out, over your father's signature, which I couldn't possibly have managed."

"That was a kind of dead end for Duke," Jansen said. "He had to wonder again if he was wrong about your father. And then he got a break, evidence that Hassam Rhamad was not the rich oil magnate he pretended to be. Duke and our people pressed hard, until we had enough on Rhamad to hang him from the nearest lamp post. Rhamad had to save his own hide. That's when we came into possession of those pictures, Miss Hargrove. That and a statement from him that the person at Hargrove Arms who'd been dealing with him was you."

"A lie, of course," Elissa said. "I was a film star by then. How on earth could I—why would I? I was rich in my own right. I didn't need money."

"You needed revenge on a man who wanted a son more than he wanted you," Jansen said.

"Sick," Kreevich said. "Sick, sick, sick."

"Duke didn't want to strike until he had you cold," Jansen said. "He was planning to reveal the whole thing in the next day or two. He didn't think he had to worry about time. He had you there in his theater, rehearsing every day, easy to keep under surveillance. How word of your danger got back to you I'm not yet certain. I don't think Duke ever told your father what he had come to believe about you. Your father would have doubted it, would almost certainly have gone to you with it, alerted you. Duke needed just one or two more small details before he hauled you out into the public, provided the Justice Department with enough to prosecute you on treason charges. But you found out, didn't you?"

"I want a lawyer," Elissa said.

"I told you there's a way," Kreevich said. "Pick up that phone and call Pat Walsh. Get him to deliver Miss Morton to us."

Elissa clearly wasn't buying that.

"Your Mr. Walsh—" Jansen began.

"*My* Mr. Walsh!" Elissa almost shouted. "He'd been out to get me for two years!"

"While you swam nude with him in Rhamad's pool? Walsh is a clever, clever man," Jansen continued. "I don't know yet how it started—unless you'd care to tell us? Oh well, a guess may be as good as a bull's-eye. He was out to get your father, international headlines that would make him a hero and a very rich man—if he was right. He made a point of meeting you, cultivating a friendship with you. Maybe he was physically irresistible to you. You almost certainly would have been irresistible to him—to almost any man, I may say."

"Thank you, sir!" It was a bitterness from Elissa.

"Somehow, during the first excitement of that affair with him, you discovered you had the same goal, the destruction of Warren Hargrove. Different reasons, but the same goal. You decided to join forces."

"Pleasant conversation after lovemaking," Kreevich said.

"Damn you!" Elissa said.

Jansen went on. "You must keep your association a secret," he said. "That brought about Walsh's apparent vendetta against you and your father in the press. You would make a lot of money selling out your father, and in the end Walsh would be the reporter of the year and also rich."

"I didn't need money, you idiot!" Elissa said. "Do you have any idea how much I'm making as a film star?"

"Revenge was what you wanted," Jansen said. "Your father had no right to want a son. It was easier than we realized at first—for you, I mean. You could come and go in and out of your father's private office, and no one would think of stopping you—the boss's daughter, the great movie star. When he was away, you could go into his office, presumably to make a phone call, to rest on the couch in his anteroom, to collect certain emergency gear you kept there like a raincoat, an umbrella. You were free as air. You had learned to copy his signature so that even an expert couldn't tell that it was a phony. You made out shipping orders and just left them in his out basket so that your father's secretary would pick them up and implement them. To coin a cliché, Miss Hargrove, it was duck soup for you."

Quist glanced at his watch. Time was skipping by.

"What happened then I can only guess. Maybe Rhamad was playing both sides of the street and warned you. Maybe someone who was his friend warned you about Duke and what lay in store for you. You didn't panic. It's not in you to panic. But the out? How many of Duke's people knew what he knew? Was it your notion or Walsh's—to blow up the theater and everyone in it, including your father, whom I expect you invited to come to that preview. Things weren't going right with the play, you wanted his advice? So you had them all there, and all that was necessary was to be ready for them. Who could set up bombs for you? No problem, you'd grown up learning your father's business, trying to be the son he wanted. You could wander around the theater anytime you wanted—just like your father's office. You were the star. No one would question you, and there'd be no one left alive afterward to remember seeing you in an odd place.

"You arranged for an explanation of why you weren't there yourself. Laryngitis. You say the stage manager sent you a doctor. You can't prove it, because you can't remember his name. The stage manager is dead. It all works fine, except for one thing. How do you get away after the bombing? How do you escape what's happening here today—questions, questions? Julian Quist, a nice, gentle, kindly man with worldwide contacts. He will understand why you want to avoid the press. He will understand that you may still be a target for someone. He will help you get to a safe place, enemy country overseas! You need help because you can't walk five feet without being recognized. It almost worked, Miss Hargrove, except that Quist wisely decided that you would be better protected by the police than by him and Garvey. You were trapped, although Quist didn't know he was trapping you. He thought he was offering you the best possible help."

"And damn him!" Elissa said.

"Did you and Walsh plan the kidnapping of Miss Morton as an escape hatch in case something went wrong?" Jansen asked.

"Or was it an afterthought of Walsh's?"

Elissa looked like a complete stranger to Quist, her eyes ice cold, her mouth a straight, thin slit. "I could send you to a film producer, Jansen, who would pay you a nice piece of change for this melodrama of yours."

"There's still a way to get yourself a lawyer, Miss Hargrove," Kreevich said.

"No!" Quist moved toward his friend, beckoned him away from the table. They walked together to the far end of the room. Quist's hand wasn't steady as he rested it on his friend's arm. "I don't think having her call Walsh is a good idea, Mark."

"You think it would be like a signal for him to make his own decision about Lydia?"

"Something like that," Quist said. "Jansen's story isn't an invention?"

"Documented. Those pictures that you didn't look at, centerfold for *Playboy Magazine!*"

"I don't give a damn about her sex life," Quist said. "The bombing, can you make that stick?"

"What we can prove is the illegal sale of arms to the enemy," Kreevich said. "This Rhamad guy spelled it out in detail to save himself. That part of it is open-and-shut. The bombing was to prevent Duke Maxwell and anyone he'd confided in from revealing it, and to keep her father from driving the last nail in their coffins. The bombing and how and who handled it is a guess, but who else? We've got enough on both Elissa and Walsh to put them away for life without the bombing."

"You believe this thing about getting revenge on her father?"

"She's that sick," Kreevich said.

"Then she wouldn't hesitate to get revenge on me for having turned her over to you," Quist said.

"Probably not."

"Then she isn't going to do anything to help us free Lydia. That would be the ultimate revenge on me, wouldn't it?"

Kreevich nodded slowly.

"You wouldn't set them free, Walsh and Elissa, put them on a plane for Libya, if they would turn Lydia over to us?"

"I would," Kreevich said. "But I doubt if Jansen and his people will. And—forty-two people are dead, Julian. What do you think their family and friends would say?"

"Would they just let Elissa go, hang on to Walsh? She can never hide from you."

"Without the aid of a plastic surgeon," Kreevich said.

"I have a feeling she might tell us where Lydia is being held if we promised to put her on a plane for the Middle East. To hell with Walsh, lover or not. That lady cares for herself more than anyone."

"I don't think Jansen will buy it. They've worked too hard and too long to nail these people. They'd be sorry about one more death, but let these two go, and there may be a whole army of deaths somewhere later on."

"Talk to him," Quist said. "While you talk to him, let me have a go at her. It's just possible she might be willing to save herself."

"I can't promise you Jansen," Kreevich said, "and I'm afraid I don't believe Elissa would follow through on any deal she agreed to make. But—let's give it a try."

"Thanks, Mark."

The detective went back to the table, and a moment later he and Jansen, Fred Vail, and the stenographer-cop left the table and walked to where Quist waited. Elissa sat motionless at the table when Quist went back and took the chair next to her.

"Willing to talk?" he asked.

"About what, Julian? You've really screwed up everybody's world, haven't you?"

"You want out of this, don't you?"

"Out?" She actually smiled at him. "Do you think for one minute Jansen is going to give me an out? You've got some kind of magic you can use on him?"

"A good lawyer for you, a chance to prove your innocence?"

"Do you think I can do that, Julian? Because you're stupider than I think you are if you do. Everything he said is exactly the way it was."

"You set the bombs at the Quatermayne?"

"I will, of course, deny it with my last breath," Elissa said. It was an oblique confession.

"You could help us get Lydia free."

"Yes, I could. I could tell you where she is right now. But I won't, Julian Quist Associates. You got me into this jam, and knowing that your Miss Morton will fry for it is something I will relish—for as long as I can relish anything."

"You could be free, among people who would protect you."

"Has Jansen told you that?"

"They're discussing it."

She laughed. "Do you think I would believe him for one minute—or your friend Kreevich? Could I believe my own friends? You heard about Hassam Rhamad? He was my friend. It's every man for himself in this world, Quist. It just happens that I've run out of gas. How does it go? When you're a loser, your friends hang you out to dry." She brought a small clenched fist down on the table. "It's over, over! The last pleasure I have in the world is to watch you sweat it out."

The telephone on the table rang. Kreevich came back from his conference to answer it. It was apparently a report of some kind from one of his men. He finally put down the phone, frowning.

"There's a fire in a building on Lexington Avenue, just a block or so away. It seems that our friend Walsh went into that building about a half an hour ago. Now he's outside with a crowd of rubberneckers, watching it burn." The corner of the detective's mouth twitched. "I think I'd like to see what's so interesting about it."

Elissa leaned back in her chair and began to laugh. "I said 'fry,' didn't I, Julian? I wonder if your Lydia will be well done or rare?"

Quist took a quick step toward the laughing woman, drew back his hand, and gave her a stinging slap across the mouth.

"Lydia!" he said to Kreevich, and both men left the room on the run.

Out on the deserted early morning street Quist and Kreevich ran east toward Lexington Avenue. A fire truck passed them, siren wailing. Around a far corner they could see black smoke pouring from the upper windows of an old building. There was a small crowd gathered outside, while firemen struggled to attach a hose to a hydrant. A man in a business suit stopped Kreevich. It turned out to be one of his men.

"Some kind of an old office building, Lieutenant," the plainclothes cop reported. "A night watchman says nobody lives in the place. He has no reason to believe there'd be anyone in it."

"But you saw Walsh go in?"

"Half an hour ago. He had some kind of a key to the front door. We were trying to figure out how to break in and follow him when somebody across the street started screaming, "Fire!" We backed off to have a look and saw the smoke. Nate Moss, my partner, went to turn in a fire alarm.

When I came back out here, there was Walsh standing in the crowd that was gathering. He'd come out in the moment or two Nate and I were missing. He's still there, just near the corner."

Quist saw him, casually watching the flames that had suddenly broken out of one of the upper windows. Everybody talks to everybody in a crowd, and Walsh seemed to be exchanging opinions with a short, stocky little man who was wearing a beret over what looked like blond hair.

Walsh saw Kreevich coming, but he made no move to run. The stocky little man to whom he'd been talking moved away a few feet, as Kreevich and his men surrounded Walsh. The reporter was smiling.

"I suppose I should have expected you to show up, Lieutenant," he said. "Your men haven't done the most professional job possible. I've known I was being tailed for the last half day or so."

"Where is she?" Kreevich demanded, his voice harsh.

"She? I don't know what you're talking about, Lieutenant."

"Miss Morton. I suspect she's in that building. Where?"

"Why would Miss Morton be in that building. She part of your follow-Walsh team?"

"You went in that building half an hour ago," Kreevich said. "You have a key."

Walsh continued to chuckle. "This building was erected during the presidency of Ulysses S. Grant," he said. "Not too many people rent space here anymore. Place is falling apart. But I have an office here. I need some place to work—write my columns—where I won't be interrupted or disturbed. I have a key so I can come and go any time of day or night I want. I needed some notes I'd left there. I got them, came out. I smelled smoke in the hallway, and when I got back out here, someone had already turned in an alarm. I stayed because I hoped it might be put out. I

176

have a valuable typewriter in there, files of notes, and records."

"Where is Lydia Morton?" Kreevich suddenly had the reporter by the front of his jacket. "Is she in that office of yours?"

Walsh laughed again. "I know I'm irresistible," he said, "but I don't think Miss Morton would go for me. She's so involved with Quist." He turned his head. "Where is Quist? I thought I saw him coming with you."

Kreevich looked around. Firemen were trying to move the gawkers farther away from the building. Quist was, indeed, missing.

Kreevich felt a moment of anxiety. Had Julian been foolish enough to try to go into the burning building to look for Lydia.

"You're under arrest, Mr. Walsh," he said, turning back to the reporter.

"On what charge?"

"Multiple murder, kidnapping, probably treason, and anything else the district attorney can dream up between now and the time you appear before the grand jury."

Quist? All his life Quist had been an intuitive hunch player. Something had stuck in his mind and was reactivated as he and Kreevich had joined the crowd outside the burning building. It happened when he saw Walsh obviously carrying on a conversation with the short, stocky man wearing a beret over blond hair. Short, stocky, and blond was the description the elevator man at Beekman Place had given of the television repairman who had brought a note from Lydia, the "Mr. Bloomfield" who had eventually tapped his phone. There were probably thousands of "short, stocky, blond" men in the neighborhood, but this one had been talking to Walsh!

Quist edged his way around the rear of the crowd of spectators. The blond man's attention appeared to be riveted on Walsh, Kreevich, and the cops. Quist moved around to a position directly behind the blond man. The crowd noise was loud, people shouting, pointing, exchanging opinions about the prospects. Quist's move was sudden and totally unexpected. His left arm went around the blond man's neck, jerking his head back. His right hand moved quickly over the man's body. He found what he was looking for, a handgun in a holster under the man's left armpit. Lydia had said there was a man pointing a gun at her. Quist spun the blond man around, and the gun was pointed between Bloomfield's eyes, not inches away.

"I'd owe you an apology if I hadn't found this, Bloomfield."

"You crazy or something? Take it and go. I got about eleven dollars on me," Bloomfield said.

"You and I are going in that building, Bloomfield, and you are going to take me to Lydia. If you don't move, right this instant, I promise you I'll blow you away with your own gun."

You could almost see alternatives in the man's suddenly frightened blue eyes.

"Now, Mr. Bloomfield. There's a chance we can all get out alive if you don't stall."

The blond man made his decision. He headed for the alley that separated the burning building from its neighbor. No one in authority apparently saw them go down the alley.

"You know I've just been doing what I got paid for," Bloomfield said.

"If you live and cooperate, that just may save you some time in the slammer," Quist said. "How do we get in?"

"Service entrance, just at the back," Bloomfield said.

"Where is she?" Quist asked. The gun was pressed hard against Bloomfield's thick neck.

"Second floor, rear," Bloomfield said. "Never make it from the front. So much smoke. Probably not make it anyhow."

"I might make dying easier for you, if you don't step on it," Quist said.

The service entrance was unlocked, untended. Inside it was pitch dark, and some smoke was already sifting down. Quist's left arm was still holding Bloomfield close.

"Lights?" Quist asked.

"Switch, just to your right, there."

"You find it, Bloomfield."

Bloomfield fumbled with his right hand, and suddenly a bare electric light bulb revealed a rickety-looking wooden stairway. They started up, slowly, because Quist refused to loosen his hold on the man or take the gun off its target. Two flights, the smoke growing thicker. Bloomfield began coughing. He stopped outside a door. There was no name on it.

"It's locked," Bloomfield said.

"You've got a key. Open it."

"We're never going to get out of here," Bloomfield said, strangling on the smoke. But he reached in his pocket, produced a key. Quist had to free him a little to let him work at the lock. Bloomfield pushed the door open—and then he spun around and lunged at Quist. Quist brought the butt of the gun down on the man's head in a crushing blow. Bloomfield stumbled to one side and fell on his face.

Quist charged into the room. He heard himself cry out. Lydia was there, sitting in an armchair, her hands tied behind her back, a wide strip of adhesive tape pasted over her mouth. Her eyes were closed. The noise from outside was so loud, she evidently hadn't heard the action at the door—or she was unconscious—or—!

Quist reached her. "Lydia! This is going to hurt, love." He took an edge of the tape and ripped it in one sharp jerk from her mouth. Her eyes popped open.

"Julian!"

"Don't try to talk. Try not even to breathe!"

179

He was fumbling with clumsy fingers at the rope that tied her hands. He didn't carry a knife. It seemed to take forever, but finally she was free. He helped her to her feet.

"I'm not sure I can walk, Julian. I've been held there for hours."

"Put your arms around my neck and hang on."

She was there, close to him, clinging to him. They struggled out of the room, into the quickly growing clouds of smoke. He tried to encourage his woman, but she didn't respond. She was hanging on, though. They managed to stumble over Bloomfield's body and reach the stairs. Better to fall down than not to go at all, Quist thought. But they didn't fall. He could see Lydia's feet bumping against the stairs as he, quite literally, dragged her. His lungs were burning. Would the second flight be possible? And then, eyes smarting, lungs tortured, he suddenly felt air. Overhead was a canopy of stars.

"We've made it, Lydia! We've made it!" He was still holding her in his arms, leaning against the adjoining building.

Then someone saw them, and there was help. Firemen with a stretcher carried Lydia out into the clear. Quist saw the blinking lights of an ambulance, and he spoke to the paramedic who was bending over the stretcher.

"Smoke—and I don't know what else," he said. "She was being held prisoner in there, bound and gagged."

"You better have yourself looked at," the paramedic said.

Quist watched them carry Lydia to the ambulance and finally turned away as it drove off. Standing not far away were Kreevich, Walsh, and the two plainclothes cops. Quist went over to them, his attention focused on Walsh.

"Your friend Bloomfield is lying in the hall just outside your office up there, Pat. Firemen may be able to get to him by way of ladders outside the windows. Let me say that, if they don't get to him, I couldn't care less."

Walsh gave him that infuriating smile. "What's happened to your humanitarian outlook on life, Quist?"

"Evaporated for the moment," Quist said. "One more thing, in case I don't get the opportunity later to let you know exactly what I think of you—" He drew back his fist and struck the reporter a smashing blow right in the middle of that smile. Walsh staggered and went down. Quist looked around at Kreevich.

The detective was looking up at the sky, star gazing. He hadn't seen anything.

Lydia looked miraculously healthy, propped up in her hospital bed. Her hands felt warm in Quist's.

"I couldn't believe it when I saw you," she said. "I thought I was in a soap opera, having one of those flashback dreams."

"We owe Martin, the elevator man at Beekman, some kind of a party," Quist said. "He described Bloomfield to me, and when I saw this short, stocky, blond man talking to Walsh outside the building, I had one of those hunches of mine. If we'd waited to break down Walsh, we might never have found you. The hunch paid off."

He had told her Jansen's story about Elissa and Walsh, their dealings and double-dealings. "What we don't know about, is exactly what happened to you."

"Sucker of all time," she said, shaking her head. "A phone call, a strange voice. Calling for you! I was to join you at Dan's apartment as soon as I could. The way things were—I knew you were there. I knew you and Kreevich were possibly questioning Elissa. This could have been one of Kreevich's men—though he didn't say so. Like an idiot, I just bought it. I didn't leave you a message because I was on my way to see you!"

"Not too idiotic," he said.

"Taxi right outside the door. I took it. I don't know how it was done, Julian—something piped into the closed in rear seat. Anyway, the next thing I knew, I was in an underground garage somewhere, still in the taxi. Walsh was there, and that Bloomfield. They made it quite clear to me the situation I was in. You would have to get Elissa free for them or I had had it."

"My poor darling!"

"I had to write that letter getting Bloomfield into the apartment. No tricks, just exactly what they told me to write, or you might not live the day out. One thing I was sure of, Julian, they would do just what they threatened to do. You or I would have just been Number forty-three—or forty-three and forty-four."

"You couldn't do anything else."

"I was kept in that garage, in the back of that taxi, until the middle of the night. Then Walsh and Bloomfield took me to the office where you found me. Bloomfield was my jailer."

"Bastard!"

"He wasn't unkind, or rough. But he was deadly, Julian. I didn't for a moment doubt what he would do if I tried anything fancy."

"Bloomfield is the one who held a gun on you when they made you call me?"

"Yes. Did they get him out of that burning building?"

"Yes—though he may wish they hadn't by the time the courts get through with him. Tonight—?"

"Walsh appeared. He told me you had chosen not to help get Elissa free. He and Bloomfield forced me into that chair, tied me, put the tape over my mouth and left me. Not too long after that I began to smell the smoke. I knew what they had in mind for me."

"You must have been scared green."

"Does it show?"

"Never. You would never show it."

"So what happens next, Julian?"

He smiled at her. "You're going to have to make yourself just as beautiful as you possibly can."

"What are we going to do?" she asked.

"*You* are going to be a star witness in one of the most sensational murder trials ever to hit the front pages of the world," he said. "I want you to outshine that Elissa bitch."

"I wish," she said, "that you had just said 'I want you.'"

"Can you ever doubt that, my darling?" Quist asked.

Except for a hunch, he might never have been able to say that to her.